Wick

Temptation

Wicked Temptation

By Caz May

First Published 2021
Paperback ISBN 978-0-6488534-7-3

Published by Caz May

© Caz May 2020-2021
Cover image from iStock
Cover editing by Caz May

To my soul sister Tina
I'm so glad you found my books
I love you girl
Make sure you share Ezekiel and don't keep our sexy
boy hidden.

Author's Preface

Hey lovely readers!

Please note there are mentions of childhood illness and related trauma in this story.
There is also other woman and other man drama and scenes throughout the story.

Also this story is set in Australia, where the age of consent is sixteen. Please do not comment on this in regard to the story in reviews and such.

Caz May
xx

Playlist

Below is the playlist of songs for this story. They're in no particular order. The Spotify playlist link is at the bottom.

1. Thinking about you-Winnona Oak, R3HAB
2. Sorrow (Conscious Sessions)-Jacob Lee
3. Shower- badly
4. Stolen Dance-Milky Chance
5. Reckless-Becoming Young
6. Miss you more than you know-Sofia Carson, R3HAB
7. Run awhile- badly
8. In your eyes-The Weekend
9. Hold you tonight- Gryffin, Chris Lane
10. Kill my time-5SOS
11. Butterfly- Crazy Town
12. Breakin' me- Jonny Lang
13. I never wanted anything more than I wanted you-Kina Grannis
14. The day you went away-M2M
15. Ignite-Alan Walker, Julie Bergan
16. Yours- Greyson Chance
17. Far away-Nickelback
18. Pretty Heart-Parker McCollum
19. Heaven-Avicii
20. I believe in a thing called love-The Darkness

Also by Caz May

Secret Santa (A Christmas Rom-Com)

My Girl Duet

Bk 1-Not my Girl
Bk 2-Still my Girl

Always Only You Series

Bk 1-Roommates Don't Kiss & Tell
Bk 2-Friends Don't Say Goodbye
Bk 3-Feelings Don't Play Fair
Bk 4-Hearts Don't Steer Us Wrong

The Mackenney Family Saga

Bk 1-Country Secrets
Bk 2-Doctor Attraction
Bk 3-Unlawful Attachment

A Holiday Romance Duet

Bk 1-Take Flight

Lockgrove Bay Series

Be Tempted Duet

Bk 1-Loathing Temptation

x

No man knows how bad he is till he has tried very hard to be good.

C. S Lewis

Prologue

Ezekiel

All night at my best mate's parents wedding I've been sneaking glances at Ava, his little sister.

Well, his not so little sister, but his sixteen-year-old sister who I've got a major jones for. Ava Castello is gorgeous, sassy and sexy as hell.

All I've thought about for weeks—even though I got my arse kicked by Ashton for it—is kissing Ava at her birthday.

Her kiss was by far the hottest most arousing kiss of my fucking life. And I'm craving another taste of her.

Thankfully, Ashton hasn't caught me staring at her either. Because he'd also see that the Z-man is threatening to poke

Caz May

out of my black slacks. I've practically had a hard on all day since I saw her walking down the aisle in the sexy navy dress. It only shows a hint of skin, but I'm thinking of what she's wearing under it—or not wearing under it—considering the straps are to thin for a bra. And my best mate be damned I'm kissing Ava again tonight.

After the speeches, and all the official wedding stuff Ava is sitting alone at the bridal table whilst Ashton dances with Tempany—their new stepsister. Making sure he's not looking at me and is to busy practically fucking Tempany on the dance floor I step up to the bridal table and lean against it.

"Av's you look fucking gorgeous," I tell her, giving her a smirk.

She giggles, replying, "You look sexy, Ezekiel."

Everyone knows I hate my full name, but when Ava says it, fuck. It fucking kills me. And Z-man throbs.

"Come with me, Av's."

I don't give her an option to say no, but I don't need to as she quickly stands up and comes around to me from the other side of the table.

She takes my hand, and a tingle races up my arm, all through my already turned on body. No one makes me feel like Ava does when she touches me.

I drag her away from the reception room to the alcove near the balcony, pushing her up against the wall.

With my hands above her head I lean into her, murmuring in her ear, "Av's, I want you, so bad."

Wicked Temptation

"Then kiss me again, Ezekiel," she practically purrs back at me. *Fuck me dead.*

I'm so fucking hard right now. Z-man is going to escape and fuck her. And god do I want to fuck her. I've wanted Ava to be mine for years, pretty much since I first started noticing chicks when I was twelve. Granted all I did when I hit puberty, was wanking, all over posters of hot chicks on my wall and over my iPad, so much so that the buttons didn't work and it smelt like jizz.

I was the idiot who wanked every damn second I could, and so much my older brother Dane told me my dick would fall off.

Tosser.

Little did he know that I lost my virginity to his girlfriend Melanie (before they got together) a couple of days after my sixteenth birthday. And after her, it was on like they do on the discovery channel.

But I couldn't have Ava then, and I've kept my distance until she was legal—thank fuck for living down under—but now I want all of her.

I now have her dress practically around her waist, and her leg is wrapped around my thigh. Z-man is hard, like steel rod hard, grinding against her pussy in the lace bodysuit she has on under her dress.

God I want to fuck her so bad right now.

My jacket is open, and her hands tug at my shirt untucking it to run her hands all over me. Her touch is electric, and I can't get enough. I don't think I could ever get enough of kissing Ava.

Caz May

But again our pash session is cut short when I feel someone yanking on my jacket, pulling me away from Ava.

I yelp in pain, biting down on my lip accidentally from breaking the kiss so abruptly. Turning around I find my best mate staring daggers at me, and Ava. She returns the dagger eyes to her brother as though she's begging him to not hurt me this time.

But I can see the anger in Ashton's eyes. I know i've fucked up again, but I can't help the way I feel about Av's. I'd risk a thousand punches from my best mate to be with his little sister. I'm about to tell him that, but I don't get the chance to open my mouth to speak before he's laying into me, pushing me down onto the ground and pummelling my chest with his balled fists.

"Ash, man, stop!" I yell at him, spit hitting him in the face.

"I told you to leave her alone, Ezekiel!" Ashton bellows at me.

"I couldn't...I...I...want her," I say too softly, worried that he hadn't heard me. I bite down on my lip, as I can't really say the words I want to.

I can't actually confess that I'm in love with his little sister. He'd not believe me, and pummel me until I couldn't walk and even though I'd risk that to be with Ava, I also don't want her to see me get hurt. I don't know how she feels about me, but if her dirty, sweet and all consuming kisses are anything to go by, Ava Castello has feelings for me too.

Ashton doesn't reply instead he raises his fist to hit me in the cheek. I'm honestly expecting more, but he's being tugged

Wicked Temptation

away and a voice behind him meekly says, "Ashton stop you're hurting him."

I know it's Tem when I manage to sit up. She's led him outside to the balcony and Ava is kneeling beside me.

"Z, are you ok?" she asks, shocking me with the nickname she's never called me before.

Come to think of it, no one has called me Z before and I like it, but I'd like Ava calling me any form of name, including my full name.

Brushing a stray hair from her cheek, I kiss her forehead. "Yeah, Av's I'm ok. Let's get back inside."

She helps me stand up, and I groan a little from the pain Ashton inflicted on me, my ribs aching like a bruise is going to colour my skin. Ava puts her arm around me, and we head into the reception room together.

Everyone is lining up for the bridge for the bridal couple to run through for good luck. Ava drops my hand, smiling at me whilst she lines up on the girls side.

I'm stuck in my own world staring at Ava when Ashton steps up beside me. Tempany joins the other side, next to Ava. Ashton glares at me, a death stare, and I nod across at Tem, asking him without words if something just happened between them. I don't think he's going to reply, but as his parents start walking through the bridge we've now created with our arms above our heads and locked together he whisper's in my ear, "I kissed her, and fuck…"

"That good huh?" I ask cockily, knowing exactly what he means about a kiss being everything and more.

"Better," he tells me when his mum reaches us.

She stops a moment to give Ava and him a hug, before taking her new husband's hand and heading out the door.

Ava is about to walk away, and Ashton stops her a moment, asking her, "Av's are still staying at Kota's?"

"Yes, is that ok?"

"Yeah, great. I'll see you tomorrow."

I watch Ava walk out the room, and don't miss the cheeky wink she gives me.

Ashton and Tempany are back at the bridal table gathering their things and heading out. He doesn't even give me another glance, to realise I'm still in the room, because he's so focused on Tempany.

He's so in love with her, even though he's denying it every damn breath.

I'm about to head out, trudging past the bathrooms out to my shitbox of a car when I bump into Ava.

"Av's what are you doing here still?

"Is Ash gone?"

"Yeah, he left with Tem before when he thought you left with Dakota."

"Oh cool, can I come to yours?"

"Av's I don't think that's a good idea. What if Ashton finds out?"

"He won't. I want you, Ezekiel."

The way she says my name makes Z-man throb in my slacks. Her suggestion is brazen, and I have no self-restraint, clearly because I reply, "Seriously Av's. I want you to."

Wicked Temptation

She doesn't say anything else but grabs my hand dragging me out to my car before I can honestly think of protesting. Her hand in mine is giving me tingles. It makes me wonder what touching more of her body, her lightly tanned skin would feel like.

Getting back to my place, it's super quiet. My parents had booked a hotel for themselves to have a night away. And my older brother is barely home these days, usually at Melanie's house.

It's me that's dragging Ava down the hallway to my bedroom. And the moment we step into my room, I slam the door pushing her against it and taking her mouth with mine in a kiss that's full of the pent up lust she ignites in me.

Still kissing me, she jumps up against my body, wrapping her legs around my arse and we stumble back towards my bed. When my knees hit the edge I fall backwards with Ava on top of me. Breaking the kiss I smile at her. Fucking grin at her, because fuck me I never thought I'd be kissing her again or have her in my bedroom on top of me.

She gives me a smile back.

"Damn Av's. You're so fucking gorgeous. But you know what?"

"What?" She says with a sweet giggle that makes Z-man throb.

"You'd look even more gorgeous out of this dress."

Again she giggles standing up and slapping a hand against my chest. Her touch, even through the dress shirt I'm still wearing sets me on fire.

27 Caz May

"Zekey, stop," she grumbles with a smirk.

My Ava is such a tease, and apparently, I have a new nickname. And I fucking love it.

With her stormy grey eyes locked on me—now sitting up on the bed, my hands by my side pressing into the mattress—she pulls the dress over her head, throwing it on the floor at her feet. *And holy shit.*

She's a fucking knockout. The strapless lace bodysuit shows the seam of her bare pussy and the hard buds of her pink nipples. Stalking back towards the bed again, I stare at her shifting back so she can climb on next to me.

"Av's," I murmur her name before kissing her. She climbs on my lap, her hands all over me, freeing me from first my shirt and then she starts to undo my slacks. I moan against her lips, breaking the kiss when she slides the zipper down, and her hand rubs my aching, hard as fuck dick. She sits back, and tugs my slacks off, throwing them aside once they reach my ankles.

And before I can think about how bad this is—but how good it feels—she's kissing me again, rocking her barely covered pussy over the front of my boxers.

Again her hands are all over me, and she slips Z-man out of the hole in the front of my boxers, stroking him as she kisses me. It's beyond ecstasy. No chicks touch has ever felt like this, so good that I could come from just a hand job. I reach down between us and tease her clit through the lace.

"Fuck, Av's," I mumble against her lips, before breaking the kiss.

Wicked Temptation

She doesn't say anything, just looks at me with her eyes hooded with lust when she yanks the buttons of the bodysuit open, so her pussy is exposed. *Fuck, I want to touch her.*

"Av's fuck. You're going to send me to hell."

She lays over me again, pressing a soft kiss to my lips, and murmurs, "More like heaven, Zekey."

And then she starts to slide her bare, wet pussy over my dick, coating it in her arousal. She's moaning, and fuck I've never heard a sound I love so much. "Fuck Av's, come for me."

And just like that she does, trembling and collapsing against my chest.

Her eyes look into mine, and she lies down next to me. I could feel annoyed that I didn't get to come, and my dick is honestly aching, but having Ava in my arms, probably for the only time it will ever happen I don't care.

"Thanks for that Zekey," she murmurs, her eyes closing. I kiss her forehead and watch her as she falls asleep. I love her so fucking much.

Rolling over, I'm shocked that Ava isn't next to me. I wonder if I dreamt holding her in my arms last night. But the way my body feels, I know I didn't dream her kisses against my lips, and I can still smell her on my dick and sheets. Ava was in my bed last night and she's gone now.

Grabbing my pants off the floor I grab out my phone to text her.

Av's you ok?

yeah but I had to go to Kota's

Oh shit yeah. Cool.

Caz May

Ashton is picking me up

Ok. miss you already Av's.

Miss you to. But…

I know. Xx

xxxx

I put my phone down on the bed, getting up again to head to the shower, and wank until my body is spent.

Last night with Ava was incredible, but we can't be together.

I have to turn off my feelings for my best mate's little sister or I'll be signing my own death certificate.

It's such a shame Ava is the only temptation I want.

Wicked Temptation

One

Ezekiel

---

1 year later

Standing in the Castello's driveway I'm staring at Ava—trying to not crack a fat—from her sexy as fuck outfit of denim shorts that brush the middle of her arse cheeks. The top she's wearing is some crop thing that's so high up her torso it's practically showing off her perfect tits and the fact she's not wearing a bra.

It's hot as blazers for early March and I'm sweating my damn balls off from the sun beating down on us, whilst we prepare to head to the city to start Uni next week.

I watch my best mate hug his sister goodbye, pulling her into a tight hug and I hate that I'm so insanely jealous that he gets to be that close to Av's.

For the past year since I kissed her I've been pining after her—whipped for her—from just a couple of kisses and a night with her in my arms. And I'm a sick fucker for wanting her and being jealous of her own brother hugging her. Granted my best mate Ashton is a sick fucker to having fallen for his stepsister Tempany when her dad and his mum got hitched last year.

They're it though...that endgame bullshit people crap on about these days.

I want my own fucking endgame—my Ava—but if I go near her, and as so much even look her way again I'm sure to be six feet under.

Ashton is fiercely protective of his little sister, and after having kicked my arse twice for kissing her, I think he'd kick my arse if he caught me even looking her way.

But right now, I need to touch her, need to feel her tits pressed against my chest one last time.

When Ashton steps back and heads around his brand new Mustang to get in the drivers seat I saunter up to Ava.

She bites her lip, watching my approach and fuck I almost cream my daks. I step up to her, hugging her and she inhales a deep breath, as though she's breathing in my cologne.

"I'm gonna miss you so hard, Av's," I whisper in her ear.

Wicked Temptation

She murmurs back in my ear, her hand reaching down between us to cup my semi hard dick. Fuck! Fuck I want to kiss her so bad right now.

"I'm already missing you, Ezekiel," she purrs, squeezing my dick and biting my ear lobe.

I hate being called Ezekiel but when my full name rolls of Av's tongue. Fuck. And fuck me.

I pull away, to tempted to kiss her when I know I have to walk away.

Walking backwards I wave at her and the rest of Ashton's family and mine. They're probably going to have a party now us boys are leaving home. I slide into the car, and Ashton doesn't even look at me as he reverses out of his family's driveway. He honks the horn and they all wave goodbye to us.

Heading out of Lockgrove Bay towards the city is giving me a mix of emotions, sadness on one hand leaving my family— and Ava—behind, but also I'm beyond elated to be heading to Uni.

Ashton still hasn't said a word, but he's gripping the steering wheel so hard his knuckles are white.

"You ok man?" I ask, not turning to look at him.

"Don't talk to me, Ezekiel. Don't fucking talk to me," he seethes, gripping the steering wheel even tighter, yanking it hard to turn a corner.

"It's going to be a long arse drive if you don't speak to me, bro."

"I told you to stay away from Ava."

"And I have."

Caz May

"Right, so hugging her goodbye with a hard on and whispering god knows what in her ear is staying away?"

"I can't deny she still turns me on, like mega turns me on, but I haven't done anything since your parents wedding. I promise, man."

"Yeah, but you've still eye fucked her. And most likely wanked thinking about my little sister, Zeke. I won't let you break her heart."

Break her heart. More like break my damn heart. I'm in love with Ava Castello.

"Who said anything about breaking her heart?"

"No one, but you're not exactly a one woman guy, Zeke."

Yeah, only because I can't have Ava.

"Nothing wrong with playing the court."

"Well, my sister isn't for playing. And if you think she is and so much as try to talk to her we'll have no business being best mates anymore."

He turns to look at me, and anger, an angry promise is reflected in his eyes. He means his words, and my heart shatters.

I've as good as lost the only girl I've ever really wanted, and if I don't rein in my feelings I'll lose my best friend, who's practically my other brother.

I need to get over Ava Castello, but I don't know if that's even possible.

Wicked Temptation

Two
Ava

W atching the boys—my brother and Ezekiel—driving away from our house, I sniff back the tears threatening to cascade down my cheeks. I already miss Zeke, because frankly, I've been missing him since our night together when my parents got married last year. Ezekiel Alessio gave me my first

Caz May

kiss and my first orgasm. And I want so desperately to give him my v-card to, but the chances of that happening are probably zero. He'll hook up with countless girls at uni because no doubt every girl he meets—single or not—will throw themselves at him.

It's not like I haven't tried to sway his attention back to me, with sexy outfits and strutting around the house when he's been over, but he doesn't even look at me.

Well, didn't even look at me, after that night he made me feel incredible. I thought I'd made myself come by touching myself but when I came on Zeke's dick I knew that was my first orgasm, and I've not been able to come like that again.

It has made me wonder how actually having sex would feel, so much so that I've contemplated searching online for a dildo to try. But I'd be mortified if my mum found out by a charge on her credit card, or when a conspicuous package turns up addressed to me.

Seeing the taillights of my brothers mustang take the turn around the corner, I rush back inside, hearing my mum calling out my name. I don't respond but run straight up the stairs to my room, flopping down on my bed and letting the tears fall onto my pillow. It's not fair that falling in love hurts so much. It's my fault though, that I'm so hurt, because I fell in love with Zeke, and he's not the type of guy to only be with one girl.

I'm startled by a soft knock on my bedroom door. I don't want to look up, and find my mum standing in my door jamb. I'm not ready to tell her about how I feel.

Wicked Temptation

Opening my mouth, still with my face against the pillow I'm about to tell her to leave me alone when I hear my best friends voice. "A, are you ok?"

I look up, and she moves into my room, coming to sit on the bed at my feet. I sit up, and she gives me a soft smile. "Have you been crying A?" she asks, making me realise I haven't responded to her first question.

"No, and um yeah."

"Is it because he left?"

"Yeah, and he..." I can't get the words out. I haven't told Dakota about what actually happened with Zeke and I. Only that we kissed. My sweet innocent bestie blushes whenever I mention sex.

"He what? Did he kiss you again?"

"No, Kota. Something else happened. Something dirty. But he ignored me afterwards, until that hug today."

"Oh, did you see him naked?"

"Yeah, Kota. And then some."

"Oh right, so um are you going to contact him?"

"I don't know whether he wants that, Kota. He doesn't feel the same way as I do."

She laughs softly, poking me in the arm. "And how's that, A?" she teases me.

"You know I'm in love with him, Kota. But it doesn't matter. I need to move on."

"Yeah, maybe. Just see what happens," she says a little to wisely for my innocent best friend.

"Yeah, I guess. Are you staying over tonight?"

Caz May

"Nah, I can't. I have a cow who's about to calf any day now. I don't want to miss it."

"Ok, fair enough," I reply with a smile, before reaching out to hug her.

She stands up after, giving me another smile.

"Message him," she tells me, walking out the door, nodding to my phone on the bedside table.

After she walks out of my room, I pick up my phone, opening Instagram to look at Zeke's profile. It doesn't make me cry, but seeing the sexy shirtless pics of him with a skateboard, standing at the pool at his house, and with a guitar over his shoulder make my whole body tingle.

Part of me wishes I'd never given into him, because now I know how good being with him feels and I'll never get to experience that again.

Wicked Temptation

Three

Ezekiel

Ashton is gripping the steering wheel, glaring at me out the corner of his eyes. He's been so uptight from the moment we reversed out of the driveway. He'd called me out on my so not platonic hug with Ava but he's clearly upset about something else because he's driving like he wants to get as far away from Lockgrove Bay as possible.

"Something else bothering you Ash? You're wound tight as man."

"Don't want to talk about it with you, right now."

"Ok, fine, burn. But get the stick out of your arse."

He doesn't say anything, just glares at me and sniffs. He's fucking crying.

"Shit man. You crying?"

He sniffs harder. "Nah, yeah," he replies sobbing and sniffing harder, wiping his arm across his face.

"You and Tem ok? You didn't kiss her goodbye in the driveway."

"Nah, said goodbye earlier this morning. But...she..." He takes in a deep breath and I'm worried he's fucked up and gotten Tem pregnant. I know he hasn't been wrapping his wang with her. And one would think he'd have learnt with the whole Fallon disaster but clearly not. "Don't tell me you knocked her up?"

He laughs then, and I'm not sure if I should be happy or if he's hiding his guilt.

"Shit nah, we just had a fight. I honestly don't even know what it was about."

"Oh, shit. How'd you say goodbye?"

Again he laughs, grinning at me. "Fucked her."

"Well, at least you let her know she's yours."

"Yeah, but that's the thing. I think she's scared I'll cheat on her."

"Yeah, can't see that happening. Tem's your endgame."

"I know that. And I've told her I love her so much, but she doesn't believe me."

"Well, bro, I'm probably not the best person to confide in about this love shit, but Tem loves you so much. You guys will be fine."

"Yeah, I hope so," he replies nodding and sighing before slamming on the brakes because we've suddenly hit inner city traffic.

"You trying to kill me or write-off another car?" I taunt, laughing and punching his elbow.

"Nah just distracted. And didn't expect so much traffic."

"Yeah me either. Do you know how to get to the new digs?"

He shakes his head and taps the GPS in the dash. "This is the address and it's apparently twenty minutes from here."

I squint at the screen, the sun glare making it difficult to see anything from the passenger seat.

"Yeah, sweet. What suburb is it in again?"

"Camberwell. Off High street or something," he replies lifting his shoulders in a shrug before following the GPS directions of telling him to make a right hand turn.

Horns honk around us and we both laugh. "Mustn't have been able to do that," I jeer. "Fucking country driver, you."

"Yeah, says the dipshit who was too scared to drive in the city."

"I don't have a death wish, thank you. I'll leave the Melbourne driving to you, and take the tram to uni."

He takes a left hand turn into a tree lined street that makes me feel like I'm back in the streets of Lockgrove Bay.

"This streetscape makes me feel like we're at home."

"Yeah, kinda cool," Ashton replies, glancing around at the apartment blocks on either side of the street.

"Is this the street?" I ask. He nods.

"What number?"

"115, and it should be up here on the left."

We both spot number 115 *'some street,'* Camberwell at the same time. It's a rather new duplex two storey townhouse and has a carpark out the front. Ashton pulls in, cutting the engine and says with a sigh, "We're here. Home sweet new home."

Unlatching my seatbelt I laugh and jeer, "Daddy's money did us well."

Ashton gets out and opens the boot to grab out our bags. We'd not had to bring much as the place is fully furnished and stocked to the brim with everything we could need in the kitchen, as well as linen and electronics. That cost extra, but Ashton could burn money now—he has that much of it—from his trust fund and the sale of his dad's castle after he went to jail at the end of last year for his abuse of Ashton and some other criminal dealings we don't have any idea about. The trial is clearly on my best mates mind because he honestly hasn't been himself since his dad's arrest. If not for Tempany I don't think we'd even be here, about to unlock our new pad to start uni next week. She's kept his temper in check, and even though they've fought about being apart I know he won't even give any other girl a second glance. He's been in love with Tempany since we were kids and fell hard and deep for her again the moment he saw her again when she moved back to Lockgrove Bay.

I honestly understand loving someone that hard, but I can't share that with him. It sucks being in love with your best mates little sister. And it sucks missing her so hard, I feel like my heart is going to fall out.

Wicked Temptation

I need to move on, and step one is walking into our new digs. Ashton's unlocked the front door and grabbing my bags I sling them over my shoulders stepping into the hallway and taking the stairs behind him. Ashton quickly claims the main bedroom—with the en-suite—and leaves me to choose between three other rooms. I choose the one that's on the opposite end of the landing to his. I need to be able to wank—and entertain girls—in peace.

Throwing my bags on the floor, I flop down on the bed and fish my phone out of my board shorts pocket. I don't know why but seeing no messages or missed calls makes my heart sink. I want to message her—but I don't—because I need to let go.

Four

Ava

For most of the day after the boys leave I lie in bed, trying to not cry every time I think of Zeke.

I don't want to be the lovesick fool pining after him when he's going to forget about me the moment he meets some new girl at uni. But I can't help it, and sitting on my bed after I

Wicked Temptation

managed to get through dinner with my mum, stepdad and Tempany without breaking down into tears I'm staring at my phone.

Zeke posted a picture on his Instagram story of him lying on his back on a queen sized bed; with black sheets. He'd hash-tagged it *#sicknewdigs* and the smile on his face is gorgeous.

It makes me think of being in bed with him after the wedding. It was a year ago, but that memory hasn't been far from my mind. I'd picture seeing him naked every time I played with myself, but nothing will ever feel as good as his touch.

I wonder if he's thought about it, and wonder if he's thinking about me now.

When he hugged me, I could have sworn I felt his hard dick against my thigh, but that was probably just wishful thinking.

Getting up from my bed, I shut my door and grab out my pj's. It's still warm, even with the slight breeze blowing through my open window, so I grab out a camisole PJ top, and short lacy bottoms. Since being with Zeke a year ago, I've been a little more brazen in my underwear choices and most of the time I don't wear knickers to bed now either, except when it's that time of the month. I slip my knickers off to pull on the bottoms and yank my t-shirt off to throw it aside. My room is a mess right now, but I honestly don't care.

Slipping the camisole on and sitting down on my bed again I wonder if Zeke also realised that I was braless today. He'd not seen me naked, but I'd seen his eyes on my boobs when I'd been in a bikini around him, and his eyes gave away the fact that he likes my boobs. But I'm sure that would be the case for

Caz May

most guys. With my phone in my one hand, I grab the teddy bear he got me for my birthday and put it in my lap whilst I cross my legs. Holding my phone up I snap a selfie, pouting my lips as though I'm blowing a kiss.

And before I can think otherwise I send it to Zeke.

His reply is instant.

Damn Av's.

I was missing you.

Missing you too. Those pj's are sexy.

I'm not wearing knickers.

You're a tease Av's. no knickers now...and no bra earlier today.

You noticed?

Oh you bet I did Av's. thought about your tits in that top all day.

Oh Av's...thinking about you naked and blushing is making me hard.

Mmm...licking my lips.

Av's as much as sexting you is fun I gotta go. Dream of me.

Never x

He doesn't reply then. And I'm regretting sending the kiss. But I'm so giddy from our sexting convo I slide under the covers—after putting my phone down—and clutch the teddy bear to my chest with one hand whilst I touch myself thinking of Zeke's dick. I shouldn't be thinking of my brother's best friend at all, but he's the only one who's ever made me feel this turned on. And it's not as though thinking of him is doing any harm, except for cementing Ezekiel further in my mind and heart more when I should be letting go of him.

Wicked Temptation

Five

Ezekiel

After sexting Ava, I'd slept well, and dreamt of her naked, and riding my dick.

Of course, that meant I woke up with a raging hard on with my hand on my dick. Quickly I stroke Z-man, still thinking of Ava and wishing it was her touching me instead of my own callous hand. I come in mere minutes, ropes of come shooting all over my bare stomach. Yanking my boxers off I wipe them over my stomach before getting out of bed and grabbing another pair from my bag.

Slipping them on, I run into the bathroom for a shower. The bathroom is fucking sick, a dual sink with brushed silver

Caz May

tap ware, and an open shower, just a single pane of glass separating it from the dunny next to it which is built into the wall somehow. There's also a corner bath that has jets and my dirty mind goes straight to fucking a chick in it.

Turning on the rain shower I step out of my boxers and under the water, soaking up the warm water like I haven't showered in forever.

It feels like I'm in a hotel, especially as there's already soap in the shower too. Grabbing it I lather it over my body, washing away the cum before I get out and wrap myself in a fluffy black towel. Black towels are manly, but I make a mental note to not jizz on them.

Back in my room I quickly get dressed, heading downstairs to find Ashton cooking breakfast, well brunch since it's like eleven am.

"Morning, Ash man," I greet him with a chipper tone, pulling out a stool and sitting on it, whilst leaning my elbows on the island counter. Turning to look at me, he's waving a spatula in his hand, and grunts at me.

"You're grumpy. Didn't you sleep or something?"

He shakes his head, flipping some eggs and bacon onto a plate and putting it on the bench in front of me. I snag a piece of bacon, chomping into it and not meeting Ashton's stare.

I'm shocked when he replies, "Nah not the best. Can't stop thinking about my fight with Tem."

"Did you speak to her last night?"

"No, I sent her a text but she didn't reply."

"Maybe she was asleep, or with ya family."

"Yeah, maybe but Av's replied when I texted her."

Wicked Temptation

"Oh, sweet. Well, maybe call Tem. It's Saturday so she won't be at school."

"Yeah true. I'm kinda worried about something else though..."

He takes a piece of bacon, biting into it as though he doesn't want to verbalise his thoughts.

"Yeah, what's that?"

"What if Tem cheats on me?" He asks, worrying his lip between his teeth. I spit the piece of bacon in my mouth out, completely flabbergasted by his stupid question.

"Yeah right dipshit. Buckley's chance of that happening."

"You don't know that Zeke. Why would she be so worried about me cheating?"

"Because you're a guy. And you're going to be surrounded by beautiful girls. And girls worry about these things."

"Yeah, I know. But I'd never cheat on Tem."

"I know, bro. And she does too. She won't cheat on you either. You two love each other and have been through so much together."

"Yeah, I'm going to go have a shower and call her."

He heads to the stairs and I call out, "Phones aren't waterproof, bro."

"Thanks for the advice, dipshit," he calls out back to me with a laugh.

I hate seeing my best mate so down about something that he shouldn't be worrying about. If Tempany cheats on him or even thinks about cheating on him, I'd want to slap her. And violence towards chicks is something I'd ever condone. And never do, so that's saying something. But it's never going to happen so it's not worth another thought.

Grabbing a fried egg off the plate I shove it into my mouth, swallowing it after only a couple bites. I also snag another piece of bacon before I head back upstairs to unpack my bags.

In my room, I throw my jocks and socks in the drawers first. I honestly don't know where to put the rest of my clothes and glance at the built-in wardrobe on the wall in front of the bed. My reflection in the glass doors looks worn out, so I flop down on my bed to have a nap. And I fall asleep thinking about fucking Ava again, whilst watching us in the mirror.

Wicked Temptation

Six

Ezekiel

All weekend I'd bummed around, settling into the new house, and playing call of duty with Ashton. It was just like being in Lockgrove Bay but without our families around. It's only been a few days but I'm missing my family, especially Dane. He's preparing to join the army and even though he's going to be in Australia for a while longer, his leaving home whilst I'm away from home to is unsettling me a little.

I should probably tell him how much I look up to him. I might be an idiot who hates his girlfriend with a passion and

Caz May

doesn't appreciate his advice most of the time but I know he'd do anything for me.

And the thought of him in the army and never coming home scares me.

Sitting in a lecture theatre on my third day of university at the Australian Institute of music, I'm trying to hold back tears thinking about my brother leaving. I'm happy to be at uni, doing a bachelor of contemporary music--it's a dream come true--but I'm already homesick. And that's from missing my family and also from missing Ava.

I want her still, and I know I shouldn't. But her texts make every day better and thinking of her and the kisses we've shared makes Z-man throb. I probably should move on, but I don't want to.

Ava is the only girl for me.

I just need to convince my best mate that I'm not going to hurt his little sister.

I'm in another world, thinking of Ava when my thoughts are interrupted by someone squeezing past my legs to sit down in the seat next to me. I'm early for the lecture, and this person—a girl—is standing next to the seat, glaring at me and then at my bag on one of the only spare seats in the lecture theatre. "Excuse me, do you mind moving your bag?" she asks, with a scowl.

I shrug, grabbing my bag and putting it down at my feet. "Sorry," I mutter, gazing over her body when she sits down next to me. Her eyes are still on me. And I taunt her, purely because I can. "Like what you see duchess?"

She smiles, laughing sweetly. And she's pretty, despite the fact that she's wearing too much makeup.

"I might, and my name is Devney," she tells me flirtatiously.

I hold out a hand to her, and she shakes it, again laughing. "I'm Zeke."

"Nice to meet you, Zeke," she says drawing out my name on her tongue. Her mouth opens and closes again like she wants to say something, which is probably no doubt *'is Zeke short for Ezekiel'?* I hate that question and shut most people down when they ask with a sharp 'no'. New people don't need to know my actual name.

"Back at you duchess. But class is about to start so you should probably stop checking me out."

"Full of yourself much?" she asks with a hint of sarcasm.

"You were staring duchess. Admit it."

"You're hot Zeke. And I'll quit staring if you go out with me?"

I scoff, then laugh. She's brazen for sure. And I kinda like it. "Oh it's like that is it, Devney?" I taunt.

"Yeah," she says, her eyes on mine, waiting for an answer.

"How do you know I'm single?"

"I don't, but I'm not going to miss the chance to ask out a hot guy. I like what i see and i get what I want."

"Fine, I'll go out with you. I'll meet you here in the courtyard Saturday at eight."

"Sounds good," she replies, turning away to focus on the lecture that we've missed half of because we've been staring at each other.

Caz May

Fiddling with the pencil in between my fingers, I watch her writing in her own notebook. And I wonder if this date will be the start of me moving on from Ava.

There's definitely chemistry sizzling between me and Devney, but Z-man isn't coming to the party, not until thoughts of Ava come to mind.

I know I need to give Devney a chance though. I need to move on from my best mate's little sister and might as well do that with a beautiful girl who knows what she wants.

Seven

Ava

*A*fter a long boring week at school, Dakota is over and we're sitting on the floor by my bed, munching on pizza and painting our nails with face masks on that supposedly clear up acne.

Caz May

Without a doubt, I need it, with my skin breaking out like crazy. It's probably because all I've done lately is indulge in chocolate and pizza to drown out my feelings with food. Yeah, I'm totally eating away my feelings for Zeke and clearly doing a shit job of it because Dakota can see right through me.

She looks across at me, stopping her flicking of the pages of the Girlfriend magazine on the floor in front of her. We'd been doing one of the stupid quizzes that are always in them about whether your crush likes you.

And I'd been non-committal with my answers. Because I'm crushing so hard on Zeke and despite his words, he doesn't like me back I'm sure of it.

It makes me really sad. And with my best friend staring at me my heart breaks even more.

"A, are you ok? Your answers are off."

"Well, yeah, Nah I'm missing Zeke."

"Oh really. Have you spoken to him?"

"Not since we texted the night the boys left, no."

She shrugs, looking back down at the magazine for a moment.

"You should move on, A."

"I know, Kota, but I don't know how to. He's obviously not missing me."

"He might be. Maybe he's just busy."

"Yeah, I guess. Probably with some pretty girl the same age as him, who loves music as much as he does. Someone perfect for him."

I put my head down, not able to meet Dakota's eyes on mine. I want to be the perfect girl for Ezekiel Alessio, but I

Wicked Temptation

know I'm not. For one I'm too young for him—kinda—and definitely to inexperienced for him when it comes to sex plus the only thing we have in common is enjoying basketball.

I haven't got a musical bone in my body, and that's his passion, even more so than basketball. We don't fit together, not opposites attract at all. And he's Ashton's best friend, a temptation that I gave in to two times I shouldn't have, and I can't give in to again, even if my heart and my body want Zeke more than my next breath.

I've been tempted to get on a train and go visit them, already missing Zeke and my brother so much after only a week.

It's a stupid thought though, and I shake it away when I realise that Dakota is speaking to me again.

"A, are you even listening?"

"Um, yeah, Nah sorry, I zoned out."

She laughs softly, a smile curving her lips.

"I said that you're pretty as, and that all the boys in our year level would jump at the chance to go out with you."

"Yeah, I guess," I reply, nodding and grabbing a handful of m&m's. Shoving them in my mouth I swallow them without biting half of them, trying to tell my traitorous brain to think of anything but Zeke, anything but his kisses that are forever on replay in my mind. But I don't want to forget how his kisses—and his touch—felt, because I don't think I'll ever feel that way again.

I know I need to move on, but easier said than done.

Eight

Ezekiel

It's a little before eight pm, Saturday night, and I'm standing in the middle of the courtyard outside the lecture theatre.

No one is in sight, and I'm actually feeling nervous about my date with Devney. I should've turned her down, but I need to move on and get Ava out of my head. And Devney is most definitely pretty.

The nervousness is most likely because I can't actually remember the last time I went on a date, and come to think of it I actually kinda haven't ever been on a date.

Completely my fault, but casual hookups had always been my thing. Countless girls had tried to turn me into their boyfriend, tried to convince me that hooking up more than once meant we were together. That didn't fly with me, and most of the time I tried to only stick Z-man inside a chicks pussy once to avoid all talk of me being in a relationship.

The last chick I'd gone for more than one round with was Lorena, and I'm regretting that choice because hurting Tempany's best friend is another strike for me with my best mate, now Tempany—his stepsister—is his girlfriend too.

Tempany thankfully doesn't hate me for hurting her best friend, but the animosity still hangs in the air, and i feel like the wanker I am.

Being totally honest though—and I was with Tempany—the only reason I didn't make any commitment to Lorena despite fucking her like four times was because my heart belongs to Ava. It's always belonged to Ava, and Z-man would belong to her as well if he ever gets to sink inside her. I know it's not going to happen—shouldn't happen—but damn I want it to happen.

I've had to resist the urge to text her—sext her to be honest—all week. The starkers pictures—with Z-man hard—are saved on my phone, and my finger has hovered over the send button too many times than I want to admit.

59

Even now whilst I'm pacing the courtyard waiting for Devney to arrive, I'm thinking about texting Ava, wondering what she's doing, what's she's doing on a Saturday night.

Images of her strutting around her house in skimpy pj's when I'd been over playing video games with Ashton flash in my mind, and Z-man jolts in my shorts. And of course, that's the very moment Devney decides to arrive, her gaze scanning my body and focusing on the lust in my daks when she greets me.

"Well, hello, Zeke," she teases, her eyes shifting from my dick to my face when she purrs my name.

The tease from Ava's lips would get another rise out of Z-man but from Devney, nothing. She might have thought his jolt was for her, but it's not, and he's tamed himself.

"Hello, Devney," I reply, leaning forward to press a kiss to her cheek. She actually murmurs from the brush of my lips against her skin, and even that doesn't get a rise out of Z-man.

I'm completely screwed, not in a good way at all. I'm so whipped for Ava, that nothing—and no one—is even getting a reaction from Z-man.

"So where are you taking me?" Devney asks, with a sweet smile.

"Somewhere we can get drunk," I reply before I can think about how horrid that declaration must sound.

Devney gulps, her hand brushing mine, as we start to walk away from the uni courtyard towards the city. I'm expecting her to reject my suggestion, but instead, she says, "Sounds great. I know a great bar not far from here."

Wicked Temptation

I follow her, a couple of steps behind her as she strides ahead of me. Her stiletto's barely make a sound on the paved street, and her short body-hugging dress rises a little as she walks, giving me a view of her bare arse. She's certainly brazen wearing a g-string under such a skimpy dress, and I like it. I need to get my head in the game to actually move on from Ava. Devney is clearly out there—one could say maybe a slut—but she's exactly the type of girl I need to get with to turn my feelings off for the girl back home that I can't have.

After way to many drinks, I'm close to being tanked, and Devney almost matched me drink for drink.

We're both beyond tipsy, and I'm surprised after our dancing—which was more like dry humping on the dance floor—that we actually have our clothes on still and are now sitting on the tram, heading back to my place.

I haven't kissed her yet, but my eyes are drawn to her lips, and the flush of colour on her cheeks. Her legs are crossed, and the dress is hitched up her thighs, practically giving me a view of her pussy in the lacy g-string underneath.

I lean into her side, whispering to her, "Devney, everyone on the whole tram can see your pussy."

She giggles, making her tits jump. I want to kiss her cleavage. And I do, suddenly licking between her tits and tasting the salt flesh. Looking up at her after, I tease, "Mmm, yummy." Again she giggles and grabs my hand, shamelessly shoving it between her legs. Leaning into her ear again, I whisper with an exhaled breath, "Wait, Devney."

Her huff of annoyance is amusing, and my drunk brain is telling me to get on with things. Curse the fact we're in public —on a packed tram—on a Saturday night. But I don't have to commit public indecency as the tram jolts to a screeching halt at my stop, and i grab her hand to drag her off, running down my street.

The front door is unlocked when we arrive, and I drag Devney straight up the stairs to my room, ignoring Ashton calling out to me from the living room.

Devney hasn't stop giggling, and pushing her into my room I tell her to shush whilst I slam the door behind us.

She yanks her shoes off, and follows me towards the bed. Falling against it I pull her down with me, and our lips crash against each other. Her kiss is good, not heart palpating good but not repulsive. She deepens it with a moan, her tongue demanding entrance to my mouth that I grant her, pushing my dick against her pussy.

Z-man is half hard. He's happy to be pashing a girl, but even though this kiss is good, it pales significantly to kissing Ava. And with the thoughts of Ava flashing in my mind, Z-man throbs, threatening to break free.

Devney obviously thinks my dick coming to the party is because of her, because she breaks the kiss glaring down at me with a smirk. I push her away.

"I can't, Devney."

Wicked Temptation

"Why not? Your dick is hard, Zeke. You clearly enjoyed that pash."

Sitting up I shift back on the bed, bumping my head against the headboard. "It was a good kiss, yeah. But nothing else is happening here."

She stumbles to her feet, scoffing at me and then she laughs with her reply, "Yeah, funny, I didn't think a guy could be a cock tease."

"I'm sorry Devney. I had a good night, but I'm..." she cuts me off, not letting me speak before she's berating me, "Forget it Zeke. I'll see you at Uni on Monday."

And before I can reply, or think about possibly saying fuck it—fuck her—she's grabbed her shoes and has slammed my bedroom door behind her.

I don't know how I'm going to explain tonight to Ashton if he asks. I'm such an idiot, not even able to forget about Ava for a damn minute to get with someone else and with Z-man rock hard there's only one thing to do.

Whipping him out of my shorts I wank, stroking him with my eyes closed whilst thoughts of Ava coming all over him fill my head.

I try to prolong the pleasure but it's only a few minutes before I come all over myself and i drift to sleep, still in my cum covered clothes and annoyed with myself for my stupidity.

Nine

Ezekiel

After shoving Devney away—and subsequently stroking Z-man until I came thinking of Ava—regret thrummed through my mind.

I know I need to move on from Ava, but it's proving to be incredibly fucking difficult.

I shouldn't be so hung up on Av's.

For fucks sake I've only kissed her twice and seen her come on my dick and I'm practically whipped as though she owns my dick and my damn heart.

Getting up early for breakfast, and slathering a couple of pieces of toast with Vegemite I take them up to my room.

I probably shouldn't be about to do what I'm going to, and I'm telling myself I'm only doing it because I kissed Devney last night, on the exact night a year ago I kissed Ava for the first time. And I want to kiss Ava again.

And honestly, I just want to see her face.

Munching on my toast, I grab my phone and bring up FaceTime, dialling Ava before I can think of a reason not to.

Her face lights up my screen, her smile wide and my heart skips a beat.

"Hey, Av's. Happy birthday for yesty."

"Hey Z. And thanks."

God, she's gorgeous.

I wish I could kiss her through the damn phone.

She's staring at me like she's expecting me to say something. And I realise I've just been staring at her.

"I miss you Av's," I tell her, giving her a wink that makes her smile at me. Her damn smile makes Z-man jolt in my jocks. "Did you do anything special for your birthday?"

She shakes her head and replies, "No just had Kota over."

"Nice," I reply nodding before licking my lips. "Wish I coulda been there to give you another birthday kiss."

She blushes, her cheeks turning a sweet pink telling me she's remembering our first kiss like it happened yesterday.

"Me too," she says softly, before pouting at me. It's like a kick in the guts, and I'm worried she's going to tell me something that will break my heart.

"Why haven't you messaged me?"

Her question stuns me. Hits me right in the feels. And my reply is a cop out, a stupid lame excuse. "It's been full on here Av's."

"Yeah," she says so sadly my heart lurches in my chest. I don't want to see her sad. It practically makes me want to rip my damn heart out. Makes me want to take the pain away and go back to a year ago to take back the kiss we shared.

It never should have happened but even though this pain of not being with her—the pain I'm clearly causing her—I don't regret kissing Ava at all.

I'm about to say sorry to her for being an idiot, but don't get the words out before she says, "Well I um have to go...I'm meeting Kota and some other friends."

Great...she's moving on. And I'm here holding my damn dick about to wank looking at pictures of her on my phone the minute she hangs up.

"Oh, cool. Can I call you again?" I ask before I can think otherwise. Calling her again would be stupid.

"I don't think that's a good idea, Ezekiel," she says with the same sad tone from before.

It breaks my heart. And I hate that I'm the dickhead making her sad.

Still, I beg her, "Please Av's. Don't push me away like you did after the wedding. We don't have to tell Ash we're talking." I'm pleading her, and can't believe the words I've just let spill from my mouth. *Let go, dickhead. You can't have her.*

"Please Ezekiel, stop. I can't. Bye." I hardly hear those words.

Wicked Temptation

She's hung up and I curse, a loud *'fuck'* leaving my mouth as I throw my phone at the wall.

It smashes.

I hear the glass shatter, but I don't give a fucking shit.

Ava just tore my damn heart out.

I fucking love her. And miss her like a damn hole in the heart. And she's pushing me away again.

Ashton knocks on my door, startling me when he opens it just a crack.

"Zeke man, you ok?" He asks, looking at me like I've got two heads.

He comes into my room. I want to shove him away, blurt out words like *'what do you fucking think,'* but I keep my lips zipped and stand up from my bed to grab my phone.

"Yeah, man. I'm fine. Just dropped my phone."

Ashton cocks an eyebrow at me, watching me pick up my shattered phone.

"You sure? Sounded like you threw it."

I laugh to cover up my guilt. And to stop myself from confessing things I can't tell him.

"Might have. But I don't want to talk about it."

His laugh follows, and he starts to head out of my room again.

"Fine. I'm having a few and playing FIFA if you're down."

I gulp before replying, "Sounds great. Nothing better to do."

'Except wank to pictures of your sister' I add in my head.

He looks at me with a scowl and I hope I didn't just say that out loud.

"Sweet man. Deal with ya hard on, and I'll have a beer waiting for ya."

I watch him bound down the stairs before adjusting Z-man in my shorts and following him out to the lounge. Hopefully, a good Sunday bro session can get my head on straight.

Ten

Ava

Sitting at a large table at our favourite hangout, I'm surrounded by my friends but I feel so low; alone. Having Zeke FaceTime me for my birthday was super sweet, and made me feel giddy that he remembered but its bought up the feelings of our first kiss a year ago. I haven't been with—nor been interested in—being with another guy since I shared my first kiss and first orgasm with Zeke.

Caz May

He set my whole body alight with longing and I know I need to move on, to hopefully find that spark with someone else but the thought of never being with Zeke again hurts.

Dakota notices my sad expression, elbowing me in the side.

"Smile A," she tells me softly.

"Yeah," I mutter looking at my best friend out of the corner of my eyes.

"Something up? You're quieter than norms."

"Zeke face timed me and he seemed really upset about something," I tell her, almost breaking into tears.

"That sucks, but he's been a dufus not talking to you," Dakota tells me in a lighter tone to try and cheer me up.

"I know Kota. But seeing him like that it hurts."

She nods, and asks, "What'd you do?"

"Told him not to call again," I blurt out, the sudden realisation that I actually pushed Zeke away again when he was begging me not to hits me hard in the chest. I start to cry, not able to hold back the tears a moment longer.

"Oh, Av don't cry. No boy is worth your tears," Dakota tells me, grabbing my hand in hers. I sniff back the tears and give my bestie a slight smile when I reply, "I know Kota."

She goes quiet then when some of our other friends sit down with us.

Dakota is concentrating on her menu and I turn to our guy friend Drake sitting on the other side of me. I wipe away the tears on my cheeks, and he smiles at me, his eyebrows cocking up when he greets me.

"Hey, Ava. You ok?"

Wicked Temptation

We'd never been close, but he was always around when we hung out in a group. And I liked him; as a friend.

"Hey Drake, and yeah I'm fine. Just missing someone," I tell him, sniffing back more tears.

"Your brother?" He enquires with a nod.

"Yeah..." I reply when I'm actually thinking, *'no his best friend.'*

Drake nods again. "That sucks. I miss my sister too. Maybe we could go out alone sometime and miss our siblings together?" He asks suggestively, giving me a wink.

"Drake...I...I um...don't..." I don't say the words I'm thinking. That I don't want to go out with him. Don't like you that way. But I don't get to say anything when he says, " You don't Date?"

"Well, um...no," I reply sheepishly, wishing he'd just stop and drop the awkward conversation.

"Oh um...ok but um...please Ava go out with me? Just one date and if it's bad I won't ask you again." He's pleading with me, and it makes my heart hurt for him.

He's not a bad guy, and I need to move on from the gorgeous Ezekiel, so I find myself replying before I can think otherwise, "Ok, fine."

"Great! I'm looking forward to it."

I don't reply, just give him and smile when the waitress comes over to take our orders.

As we're eating Drake keeps smiling at me and I can't help but think that maybe moving on from Zeke might not be so bad.

71   Caz May

I could do worse than Drake Peters. He's my age, cute, plays basketball and clearly likes me.

I don't hate him, so maybe this date will be the first step in moving on from the guy who's had my heart for way to long.

Eleven

Ezekiel

Ever since Devney left my room after our date I've been avoiding her, even in class I've made a conscious effort to avoid her. I'd even sat at the front of the lecture theatre for the classes we had together.

When she walked past today she glared at me, hurt flashing in her eyes.

I feel like a right wanker. She's pretty and seems like a nice girl. And I honestly can't remember much from our night out.

I was too tanked and kinda just blocked Devney out with thoughts of Ava.

Caz May

She'd looked so fucking sad when I called her for her birthday and I hated seeing her like that. It breaks my heart and honestly seeing any chick hurting gets to me, especially when I'm the cause of the hurt and they look at me like I've ripped a hole in their heart. I feel like such an arsehole, as all I seem to be doing lately is hurting every chick I'm with.

I broke Lorena's heart when I told her I didn't love her back and couldn't be her boyfriend despite fucking her four times. And now I've broken Devney's heart as she's clearly upset with me.

I never should've agreed to the damn date, but I need to move on from Ava. Our hearts are broken, by each other, for each other. I don't think mine will ever be repaired or beat for someone else the way it does for Ava Castello.

I barely hear the professor for the entire lecture—to much in my own damn head—that I'm a little taken aback when the lecture is over and everyone starts filing out of the classroom.

They're all leaving like a herd of elephants and soon there's hardly anyone left in the room. I'm only taking my time because I don't have any other classes for the day. And I'm hoping to avoid Devney, even though we probably need to talk about the aftermath of our date and the kiss we shared.

Standing up I sling my bag over my shoulder, not looking where I'm going as I stalk out of the lecture theatre.

I feel low, physically and mentally exhausted. I've never felt so weak before, like I could sleep all arvo and then all night.

Not since I was five have I felt so low. It scares the fucking shit out of me but I don't want to go there, don't want to think

Wicked Temptation

about that horrible time. There's no way that's happening again.

Clutching a hand against my chest I slowly walk out of the lecture theatre and bump into a chick, copping a good feel of her tit.

Looking up I'm face to face with Devney and we both jump apart in shock.

"Damn, Sorry duchess. Didn't mean to cop a feel."

"Whatever, Zeke," she snaps, her tone soft, before a slight smile creeps onto her face, confusing me.

I'm at a fucking loss for words. She looks really pretty, wearing far less makeup than usual and her hair is up, highlighting her angled face.

"Can we talk? Grab a coffee?" She asks with a hopeful tone.

"Now?" I query, wondering if I should be contemplating drinking caffeine when my heart is racing, again.

"Sure, why not," I reply shrugging as I follow her out of the building. We don't talk as we head to the campus coffee shop. She just keeps looking at me out of the corner of her eyes, opening her mouth like a damn carp like she wants to say something but then thinks the better of it.

Getting to the coffee shop, we order. I go for an iced chocolate instead, hoping it will freeze my heart so I don't have to hurt anymore.

We take a seat—with our drinks in hand—and she's still eyeing me.

"So whats up, duchess?" I taunt, taking a sip of my drink.

Caz May

"Can you quit it?" she snaps at me, taking a big gulp of her latte.

She's being really abrupt with me. And I get it. I've been a dick to her. I deserve it.

"Devney, I'm sorry ok," I apologise, stumbling on her name and wondering if I could taunt her more with duchess. "You're gorgeous, but I'm in love with someone else," I admit, feeling my heart pound in my chest just thinking of Ava.

"So you've got a girlfriend?" Devney queries, again taking a sip of her latte. She's not going to like my answer but it's the truth.

"No...I don't. But I'm..." I can't even get the words out. They hurt so fucking much.

"What Zeke?" Devney probes, looking straight at me like she's trying to pull the answer out of me through my eyes.

"I'm in love with a girl I can't have."

She gets annoyed, her tone angry when she blurts out, "Then move on."

I clench my fists, my own anger flaring. "I'm fucking trying, believe me. But I can't get past kissing someone."

She doesn't reply at first, instead, she winks at me and I'm damn confused, even more so when she teases, "Well I'm still down if you want to try."

"Um, ok," I mutter, unsure of what else to say to her again brazen proposition.

"You're hot, Zeke," she tells me with a teasing smile.

"Thanks. And yeah thanks for the offer. I'll think about it." I won't but I'm not going to tell her that. I'm hoping that maybe if I spend more time with her I'll fall for her. It's probably not

Wicked Temptation

going to happen but I'm going to try, starting with something she won't expect.

Leaning forward I give her a kiss. She smiles against my lips, letting out a little moan. But I'm honestly not feeling it.

Normally kissing a chick would get a rise out of Z-man but kissing Devney honestly feels like kissing a dead fish. She's gorgeous but she needs some kissing practice.

I break the kiss—before I gag—and stand up, still clutching my iced chocolate in one hand. She follows the action, and this time I kiss her cheek.

"I'll catch ya later, duchess."

She smiles at the nickname this time, and I can feel her eyes on me as I walk away.

I think I'm making a big mistake.

My mind is spinning with thoughts the whole way home on the tram. Normally—in the past—kissing any girl would get a rise out of Z-man. But since kissing Ava, no other kiss has made me feel alive. Her kiss set me alight and not being able to be with her is going to be my downfall.

I want Ava. I fucking need Ava, but I can't have Ava. Devney is willing to make me forget and I know I should let her in but it seems impossible to let go of the one person who's had my heart for as long as I can remember.

I've only been a tool about her because I can't exactly tell my best mate I'm so in love with his baby sister it hurts. And

Caz May

even more so, I can't tell him all the actual dirty things I want to do to her; with her. He'd cut my balls off and then beat me to a pulp.

Getting home, I absentmindedly—out of habit—check the letterbox. There usually isn't anything inside but today there's one letter; a card. And I know exactly what it is. My hand is shaking from just holding it. I don't want to open it. Opening it acknowledges that it's happening and that my heart is going to be even more broken than it already is. But I need to rip the bandaid off to face the wound. Sliding the card out I look at the fancy lettering. It makes my heart lurch in my chest to read the words.

Dane's Pissing off to Puckapunyal Party
Saturday 9th April
6 pm onwards
Lockgrove Bay Hotel
Wear Army threads

Slipping the invite back into the envelope I nearly rip it. Seems a little uncanny that reading it has practically ripped my heart out. I don't tell him, like ever, but I love my older brother more than he'll ever know. I haven't always shown him that, and he probably has no idea how much I look up to and admire him. He was always there for me growing up and now I'm scared about losing him when I need him the most.

Walking inside I find Ashton is in the kitchen, cooking again. I don't know when my best mate became such a whizz in the kitchen—but he's a damn good cook—and I'm never

Wicked Temptation

starving with him around. If I were living on my own, I'd be drowning in brown Macca's paper bags and pizza boxes.

He hears me come in, parking my backside on the breakfast bar stool. He turns to look at me, with a smirk.

"Hey man. How was your day?" He asks.

I shake my head, looking down when I reply, "Kinda shit. Ran into that chick I hooked up with again. She still wants me." I'm blurting out words but my thoughts are still spinning. I've hardly confided in Ashton about anything lately and bottling it up isn't helping at all.

"Oh shit. Wasn't the hookup good?"

"Well, yeah, Nah we only pashed," I tell him, feeling an odd sense of relief rush over me.

His eyes boggle at me.

"Serious? Was it a case of beer goggles?"

"Nah, she's hot but she's um...not..." I cut my words off, thankfully as I was about to say, Ava. I don't need another beating right now.

"She's not what?" He asks shrugging with confusion on his face.

"Nothing, forget it. More important things to worry about."

Again he gives me the what the actual fuck are you talking about stare, and asks, "Like what?"

I put the envelope down on the bench in front of me a moment. Ashton glares at it, but doesn't say anything.

"Dane's farewell next weekend," I say, holding up the invite.

"Oh shit. Well, yeah, we'll have to head home for that shindig for sure."

"Yeah," I reply, sliding off the stool and grabbing a beer out of the fridge before heading up to my room.

Taking a few sips, I lie back on my bed and open Instagram on my phone, clicking straight through to Ava's profile.

Every picture of her is gorgeous.

Her luscious blonde hair down, her pouting her kissable lips and wearing next to nothing.

Even the ones where she's playing basketball, hanging from the hoop or hanging out with Dakota she shines, and my heart aches as well as Z-man tenting my shorts.

I'm angry at myself that she still has this effect on me, and I've not even fucked her.

God, I want to fuck her into next year.

I yank Z-man out of my shorts, and with one hand wrapped around him, I jerk off, scrolling through Ava's pictures and reels until I come all over myself.

Wicked Temptation

Twelve

Ava

S tupidly I'm nervous about my date with Drake. I've practically thrown half my wardrobe over my bedroom floor, and I'm still standing in the middle of my room in my underwear when Drake is due to pick me up any minute.

I don't have time to care anymore—and I don't know why I even care anyway—so I tug on my distressed black skinny jeans and a loose-fitting white 'The Darkness' t-shirt. Drake probably won't think I look particularly hot, nor will he get the band reference but it's my favourite t-shirt and my most comfortable outfit. Curse looking good for him.

I grab my phone and some cash from my purse. I shove them in my back pocket and bound down the stairs when I hear the doorbell ring. I wanted to avoid the whole meet the parent's thing, but Matias—my stepdad—is working from home, since mum is doing some extra shifts at the hospital and he's opened the door to Drake.

I stop next to Matias, giving Drake an awkward smile.

"Hey, Drake," I greet him, taking the flowers he holds out to me. They're daises and I'm not much of a flower girl, but I give him a nod when I take them. He's gone all shy, and says, "Hey, Ava. I um...didn't know what to get you."

"That's ok. I like them. Just give me a minute to put them in water and we can go."

"Ok, sounds good," he replies, looking at Matias still standing in the doorjamb as I head to the kitchen to put the flowers in a vase on the bench. Mum will like them.

Getting back to the door, I take Drake's hand. Matias gives me a kiss on the forehead.

"Have a good night, honey," he says, making my heart beat wildly in my chest. I want to hug him. He's been more of a dad to me the last year than my own father ever was. He loves Ashton and me as though we're his kids and I love him just as much.

I hadn't even been to the jail to see dad since he got arrested and refused bail before his trial in a couple of months.

Wicked Temptation

He never made an effort to see me or cared about my life, and when I found out all the pain he inflicted on my brother I honestly didn't even want to look at him. Ashton's anger issues make sense now, but I still hate to see him hurting Zeke.

Following Drake out, I sigh, annoyed at myself that I'm about to go out on a date with another guy and I'm still thinking about Ezekiel. He owns my heart, but I need to focus on this date and moving on. It's going to be a challenge, especially in a few weeks when Ashton and Zeke will be home for Dane's farewell party. I'm having mixed feelings about seeing Zeke again.

I've worked out my outfit for the farewell party and I'm only wearing it for him even though it's crazy to do that.

I realise that Drake is talking to me, and I nod, unsure of what he said. We slide into his car, and he drives off, not saying anything else.

My stomach is in knots. I feel like I'm going to be sick.

He drives in silence, concentrating on the road ahead, and I clutch my t-shirt against my stomach to try and curb my nausea. His silence is making me feel uncomfortable and I'm glad when we pull up outside Enzo's and he cuts the engine.

He gives me a smile.

"You sure this is ok?" he asks.

"Yeah, pizza is my fave," I tell him, getting out of the car before he can be all chivalrous.

Once he's out of the car he walks around to my side and takes my hand. It's soft and clammy in mine, and I have to resist the urge to snatch my hand back in disgust.

It doesn't give me a rush, no tingles racing up my arm and through my body; like when Zeke touches me.

I don't know what it is about Ezekiel Alessio that gets to me so much. Even just thinking about him—when I shouldn't be—makes me feel all tingly; everywhere.

I follow Drake inside and to the booths at the back. He drops my hand and we slide into the booth seats, on opposite sides. I know what I'm ordering but I still grab a menu, staring into it and wishing I could be anywhere but on this hella awkward date.

Drake puts his menu down and gulps so hard he makes a sound. I don't think I'm going to be able to keep food down with how nauseous his weird actions are making me feel.

I have to order something though or he's going to think I'm one of those girls who doesn't eat because all I care about is my appearance. I honestly don't and prefer how I look without makeup, rather than with it. My go to look is mascara, BB cream and lipgloss.

Drake breaks my thoughts.

"What're you getting?" he asks, glaring at me when he puts his menu down.

"Was thinking a Margherita pizza and a sprite. You?"

"I was going to go a Margherita pizza and a choccie shake."

"Why don't we share a pizza then? I'm not that hungry."

"Sounds ripper," he replies, hollering to the waitress to come over with his hand.

He rattles off our order and she smiles before she walks away.

The silence between us is killing me, so I ask, "How's basketball going?"

"It's alright. Ahmed is nowhere near as good of a captain as Ashton was."

"Yeah," I reply, sullen from missing my brother.

"Is he playing at Uni?" Drake asks with an eager smile. It makes me wonder for a moment if he's only going out with me to get an in with my brother to play uni basketball.

"I don't know. He's doing sports science or something."

"Sounds good," Drake replies with a nod when our drinks and pizza arrive at the table.

We each take a slice of pizza and eat in silence for the rest of the date.

I'm surprised that he pays and follows me to my front door at the end of the night.

"Thanks, Ava. I had a good night."

"Me, too, Drake," I tell him with a smile I'm really not feeling, but I'm trying to be polite. He's staring at me, his eyes darting to my lips.

Before I can say, 'no please don't' he's leaning forward to kiss me.

I kiss him back, giving in to the moment because I'm quite frankly horny and miss kissing someone. The kiss is good, but nothing compared to kissing Zeke.

Pulling back from Drake's kiss, he's smiling at me again.

"We should go out again sometime," he suggests eagerly.

Caz May

I want to say no, but my brain reminds me that I need to move on and Drake is a nice guy. He's not Ezekiel *'sexy as fuck'* Alessio, but he's still cute and good for me.

"Yeah, that would be nice," I reply, trying to lace my tone with sincerity.

"Great! I'll see you at school on Monday," he tells me before walking to his car, waving at me as I head inside.

I run upstairs to the bathroom to have a shower.

My thoughts wander to Zeke and again I touch myself thinking about making myself come on his glorious dick.

Wicked Temptation

Thirteen

Ezekiel

Ashton is flooring the mustang as we head out of the city, going home to Lockgrove Bay for the first time since we started Uni just over a month ago.

The tension between us in the car is thick, and I'm on edge. It feels like anything I say will make him bite my head off. I'm worried about seeing Ava again, as I'm sure she'll look gorgeous and keeping my hands off her after not seeing her is going to be a challenge. I don't know how I kept my hands off her for an entire year after Ashton's parents' wedding.

She's always been a walking, wicked temptation.

Caz May

The last month since we left though, and we've been apart but talking behind Ashton's back I feel closer to Ava than I ever have. And that scares me. I'm also worried about saying goodbye to my brother. He's only going to be three hours away in Puckapunyal but I don't know when I'll get to see him again and the thought of him missing out on family events, like my twenty-first birthday hurts so much.

I still remember getting really drunk at his twenty-first, and dive-bombing into the pool, splashing all our guests and getting reprimanded by Dad for my careless behaviour. Being only fourteen I shouldn't have been drinking, but I'd snuck a beer for myself and Ashton. It went straight to my head. I'd been watching Ava that night too. It was the first time I'd really noticed how pretty she was.

Z-man had been making his appearance known with wet dreams and spontaneous erections for a while, and that night —maybe because of the alcohol—I got my first stiffy looking at Ava Castello. I felt like a dirty little boy for sure. She was only twelve, and I shouldn't have been thinking about her like that, but from then on my feelings for her only grew, hitting me head on when I finally kissed her at her sixteenth birthday. And I want to give Ava Castello all her firsts, even if I don't deserve any of them.

We're out on the freeway now, and Ashton has the cruise control on. He looks across at me, breaking the silence and tension between us when he asks, "You ok man?"

I can't voice all my thoughts, so focus on my thoughts about Dane.

Wicked Temptation

"Nah, I'm gonna miss him so much. I know since we've been gone this last month or so we've only chatted a couple of times but he's my big bro."

"Yeah, it sucks man, but for the meantime, he's still gonna be down under. You'll still get to speak to him."

"Yeah, I know. I'm kinda looking forward to seeing Av's again tonight," I blurt out without thinking about what he might think. He'd be shocked if he was a mind reader.

"Don't even go there, Ezekiel," he threatens, his eyes locking on mine darker than normal. "How many times do I have to tell you my sister is off limits?"

I laugh at his question, shaking my head. "Infinity man," I tell him.

He doesn't laugh back when he replies, "Seems so."

I've clearly crossed the line again, and the fact that he's driving is the most likely the only reason I'm not getting pummelled again for my comments about Ava.

"Are you looking forward to seeing Tem?" I ask to steer the convo in a different direction that will stop me from thinking about seeing Ava in a couple of hours.

"Definitely," he says happily. "Phone sex isn't the same."

He blushes with his words, and I laugh before taunting him, "Eww...man. I don't need that visual especially as I've heard your moans at night."

This time he does laugh. "Sorry man. But clearly, you need to get some action. Your hand will fall off with how much you've been wanking."

He's eyeing me, and I hope he hasn't heard more than my moaning. Hasn't heard me calling out Ava as I've come.

Caz May

"Don't act like Dane," I snap. "And well..." I cut my words off, not wanting to say anymore or to confess that I've been wanking and thinking about Ava whilst looking at pics of her on Facebook and Instagram.

Just thinking about her now is making Z-man throb. And curse it, I'm going to fucking kiss her again tonight.

And maybe even tell her how I feel about her.

Fourteen

Ezekiel

Walking into my brother's farewell shindig—at the pub —my eyes scan the room for him, but also for Ava.

She'd mentioned something in a Facebook post about her outfit and I've been dying to see it for weeks.

Dressing up in army gear is making me feel macho, and like a badass who honestly couldn't give a fuck about consequences.

And consequences be damned because when I spot Ava across the room, my camouflage pants do absolutely nothing

Caz May

—zilch—to camouflage the raging hard on her outfit elicits from Z-man.

It's a long-sleeved khaki green bodysuit that shows off her sexy arse cheeks. She's paired it with a black utility belt and thigh-high almost sheer black stay-up stockings. Her hair cascades down her back and I'm salivating thinking about pulling her close to me, grabbing her hair and cupping her arse in my hands. She spots me to, and we're drawn to each other from across the room.

When she reaches me, scanning my outfit—and hard on—she murmurs softly.

"Hey Zekey," she purrs at me. Z-man is about to break free. *Fuck.* And fuck I've missed her.

"Damn Av's, baby," I say in greeting, taking in her outfit again. "This outfit is sexy."

She stretches up on her tiptoes in her black high heeled boots to whisper in my ear, "I wore it for you."

"Mmm...I fucking love it Av's. Come here."

I grab her hand, pulling her body against mine as I drag her around the corner. Her hand brushes against my light khaki green t-shirt, her touch instantly warming my skin underneath. I wrap a hand around her waist, pulling her even closer, my eyes dipping to hers from under the brim of my camouflage cap.

"Kiss me, Av's," I tease, sticking my tongue out. She giggles, her tongue darting out from between her lips to tease me back.

"Fuck, Ava, please...just fucking kiss me, baby."

Wicked Temptation

Again she giggles before I take her mouth with mine, kissing her so hard she murmurs like I've hurt her, but then she's kissing me back, practically trying to climb me to get closer.

This kiss is even better than the other two we've shared. Months of pent up lust igniting the connection between us.

Kissing Ava sets my whole body alight.

Her hands are all over me, about to undo my belt buckle when I hear his bellowing voice, "What the fuck, Ezekiel!"

Ava breaks the kiss, stepping away from me to face her brother who is furious, so much so I can see the anger rising in his coloured cheeks and the steam pouring out his ears.

I've fucked up, I know that.

I don't know how I'm getting out of this still walking, but I'm hoping to play my best mate.

"What's up, Ashy?" I jeer, knowing he hates when I tease him with his childhood nickname.

"What's up? What's up is you mauling my fucking sister, you fucking tosser!"

"So, Ashy? She looks sexy...and we were just playing."

He launches at me, his fist balled when he punches me right in the jaw.

"You fucking wanker, Ezekiel!"

I taunt him back, "You're the only wanker here, Ashy. Av's wanted to kiss me. Deal with it, arsehole."

He punches me again, and I fight back.

"Hit me again, arsehole. Won't stop me from kissing...and fucking Ava."

"You wouldn't dare! You're a fucking manwhore, Ezekiel. I fucking hate you."

He chokes on the words, and they hit me in the feels. Ashton hating me would be worse than having my heart ripped out. I love him like a fucking brother.

"Damn bro, that hurts. Just get a damn grip. I'll lay off, I promise. Just don't hate me."

He's still seething, about to lay into me again when Tem comes up next to him with a drink.

She whispers something in his ear which instantly calms him down. He wraps an arm around her waist, pulling her closer and kissing the side of her head.

I look at Ava who has tears stinging her eyes. I've put them there, and I feel shitballs about it.

Ashton takes a sip of his drink, before looking at Ava standing next to me.

"Go and put some pants on, Ava. Ezekiel, the dirty fucker might like seeing your arse but no else needs to."

She nods at her brother, muttering, "Fine," under her breath, sniffing back her tears when she rushes out of the room.

I don't have anything else to say to my best mate, so I head to the bar to grab a drink.

I'm losing everyone I care about and wish it was me leaving for the army instead.

But that's not even a possibility in my case, so all I can do is drown my sorrow in beer and hope I wake up in a ditch camouflaged by dense bush; if I wake up.

Wicked Temptation

Fifteen

Ava

"**F**ine," I mutter under my breath, leaving the room in a huff to go and find Dane to say goodbye. I feel horrible for wanting to leave so early, but I know Dane won't mind.

I find him standing at one of the tables near the back, sipping a beer. Walking up to him, I try to smile but fail.

"Hi Dane, I'm heading off. I just wanted to come over and say goodbye."

Caz May

He smiles at me, the same signature smile that his younger brother has, an Alessio brothers thing, clearly.

"Thanks, Ava. Any reason you're leaving early?"

"I'm just tired, and have heaps of homework," I tell him, biting down on my lip. Dane has always been so sweet, such a genuinely nice guy but he towers over me—more than Zeke does—and he's always made me nervous.

"You sure Ava? You seem upset about something." He's looking at me like he can see right through my fake smile. And I decide to probe Zeke's big brother for some answers.

"Has Ezekiel ever said anything about me?" I ask, cautiously.

"Nah, why? Did he hurt you?" Dane asks, eyeing me as he takes a sip of his beer.

"We've um...kissed a few times, including just before. But he..." I cut my words off. I don't know if confessing what's happened with Zeke and I to his older brother is a good idea after all. "Forget it...you're his brother."

Dane laughs then, a deep chuckle that makes his chest vibrate. His demeanour seems angry though when he says, "I'll kick his arse for you, Ava. If you want me to."

I shake my head.

"Nah, it's ok. Ashton has done that. But I don't want Zeke to get hurt."

Dane nods, giving me a cheeky wink when he teases, "Oh... you've got feelings for my little brother, huh?"

"Yeah, please don't say anything Dane. With him in the city, I need to move on, and I'm trying."

He smiles at me again.

Wicked Temptation

"Our secret Ava. I promise. Thanks for coming tonight."

"No worries. Good luck in the army."

He pulls me into a hug that makes me feel like crying.

"Thank you," he tells me when he pulls back. "And I'll keep our secret but knock some sense into my little brother too."

"Thanks, Dane. Enjoy the rest of your night," I tell him, as I give him a smile whilst I walk off to find Dakota.

I find Dakota standing outside against the wall, playing on her phone. Stepping up to her I ask, "What are you doing Kota?"

"Oh, just taking a break. It was hot in there."

I snigger at my best friend. It wasn't hot—temperature wise—in the pub, but Dakota hates crowded places and drama.

I'm worried about telling her about what happened with Zeke again, but it's on replay in my mind. I also don't want to go back inside.

"Yeah, you wanna go?"

"Do I ever," she chants, tucking her phone in her pocket.

We walk home in silence. Dakota keeps looking at me out of the corner of her eyes and scuffing her Converse on the footpath as we walk.

When we get back to my house, we head straight upstairs to my room, and without thinking I strip from the sexy army outfit, throwing it to the floor like it's on fire. I pull a nightie over my head and flop down on my bed.

Dakota has put on some pj's as well and sits next to me on top of the covers.

She looks at me—whilst I'm trying to hold back my tears—and asks, "A, are you ok? You're really quiet."

"I'm fine," I snap, sniffing back the tears that are threatening to fall down my cheeks.

I'm so angry at Ashton for the way he treated Zeke. But Zeke's kiss is still on my mind, and I can still feel it on my lips, and his body against mine.

"No, you're not," Dakota snaps. "Did you see Zeke?"

I grab my 'Hello Kitty' throw pillow, holding it against my chest.

"Yeah," I say, my words muffled into the pillow before I look up again when Dakota slides under the covers next to me, sinking into the bed with a sigh.

"And what? Did he look good?"

"Hot as hell. His usual sexy as hell self."

"Yeah," she says with a laugh. "Boys in military gear huh?"

"Exactly, but Ezekiel in it. And…." I cut my words off, thinking of Zeke in his sexy army outfit and his hard dick pressing into my stomach.

"What? Did something happen again?"

"Yeah, he kissed me again. And Kota I can't even tell you how his kisses make me feel. All hot and tingly, like I want to tear my clothes off."

His words of wanting to *fuck me* reverberate in my mind.

"Eww, A. Gross."

I laugh at my best friend's innocence.

"So not gross, Kota. You'll know one day," I tease her.

Wicked Temptation

"If you say so," she says blushing. "What about Drake?"

"No comparison at all, but I have to move on from Ezekiel, so it's not like I have a choice."

"Maybe things with Drake will be like that, eventually?" she suggests, having no idea that no one will ever make me feel the way Zeke does.

Being with Ezekiel Alessio is like playing with matches. It leaves me feeling damaged, good but bad.

"Yeah, I doubt it. Anyway...enough talk about my love life. I saw Keith staring at you in P.E the other day."

"Really?" she asks, raising an eyebrow at me.

"Yeah, Kota. I heard he likes you. Like likes you."

"Oh," she mutters, biting down on her lip.

I playfully punch her in the side.

"You're silly Kota. I think you should make a move on him."

"Nah, I'll leave that to him," she tells me.

"Whatever you say. You hungry?"

"Starved."

"Yeah, let's get a snack," I reply, flipping the sheets off and climbing out of bed to head out to the kitchen for a late night snack.

Sixteen

Ezekiel

All I've thought about for the past couple of weeks since going home for Dane's farewell is the hot kiss I shared with Ava.

Ashton didn't talk to me for the rest of the weekend, and the entire drive back to the city. I'd wanted to apologise, but at the same time, I'm not going to apologise—again—for kissing Ava. I'm drawn to Ava as though magnets are lodged in our hearts that pull us together.

But despite that feeling, I'm brushing that aside to side with my best mate, my brother from another mother.

We were talking again, having bonded again over a few beers and a few games of Call of duty where I let him kill me, repeatedly, on purpose. It wasn't a big grand gesture, an apology with words but it was Ashton and me, apologising to each other in our way.

With Ava constantly on my mind, I've been slacking off with uni work to, especially the major assessment of writing a song.

I'd invited Devney over—to help me—and she's sitting on my bed, cross-legged with her notebook on her lap and twiddling a pen between her fingers. I'm watching her, biting on her lip as though she's deep in thought.

"Duchess?" I ask, making her look up at me.

"What Zeke?" she asks, with anger in her tone. I called her Duchess again, even though I know she hates it. Getting a rise out of her is surprisingly fun. And I need to take the edge off somehow.

"Wanna take a break? You've been staring at that blank page for half an hour."

"You've been playing that same slow melody, Zeke. You're a sad sack of shit."

"Yeah, nailed it, duchess. You got me in one. Make me feel better?" Her eyes light up, and I know it's wrong to be leading her on, but I'm fucking horny. My hand isn't doing the damn job anymore, and Devney is willing to service Z-man and she's pretty.

"And how might I do that, Zeke?"

I chuckle, putting my guitar down by the bed, before leaning forward and whispering against her lips, "Suck me, duchess."

I'm expecting her to shove me away with her maddening defiance, but she doesn't. Instead, she closes the little distance between us with a kiss, crashing her lips to mine and pushing me down on the bed.

I have to admit Devney can kiss a guy good when she wants to. Her lips against mine isn't soul shattering like kissing Ava is, but I'm not repulsed, and Z-man is starting to stir in my daks.

That could probably be because I'm thinking about Ava's kiss, but Devney doesn't need to know that.

She breaks the kiss, eye fucking me as she shoves a hand into my shorts, and starts stroking Z-man. Her grip is strong, and sure of herself, as though she's given quite a few hand jobs in her life. But I don't want a handy. I want a gobby.

"Aren't you going to suck me, Duchess?" I taunt, smirking at her.

She doesn't say anything, just yanks my shorts down to my knees. And before I can even say anything or push her away she takes Z-man between her lips.

And holy fuck the girl can suck dick.

Her tongue licks over my tip, and she takes my dick in and out of her mouth.

It feels fucking good, so fucking good.

I close my eyes and imagine Ava is sucking me off instead.

Wicked Temptation

I have to press my lips together to not let the wrong name slip out of my mouth as the pleasure builds in my balls. I'm honestly tempted to just keep Devney around, and string her along to get the occasional gobby.

I snap my eyes open when Devney pulls back completely. "Why'd you stop, duchess?" I taunt, shoving her face back towards my dick harshly.

I'm painfully hard now, and I need to come.

"I want to come down your throat, duchess."

She takes my dick back into her mouth, and deep throats me. I explode into her mouth, shooting my load all the way down into her throat.

When she stretches up to kiss me after, I shove her away. "Seriously duchess?"

"What? I can't even kiss you now, after I sucked you off."

"Nah, I don't need to taste my jizz thanks."

She pouts, then scowls at me.

"Oh well maybe you could return the favour?" she asks with a seductive tone whilst brushing her finger across her lips to collect the drop of my cum still on them.

"Yeah, not now, Devney. I'm not really into eating a chick out. Another time."

She turns red, sudden anger flaring as she stands up from the bed. Her hand is outstretched towards me and I think for a moment that she's going to slap me. But she doesn't. She's just majorly pissed off and quite frankly she looks hot all pissed off with me.

"Seriously Zeke! You're an arsehole!" she bellows, throwing her hands up in the air. I let out a sigh of relief that she's not slapping me.

"Whoever this girl is that you're in love with honestly I feel sorry for her."

I don't reply. There's nothing to say. Nothing good that is.

Devney continues, with her hands on her hips. She's so sassy when she's angry and I want to laugh, but I'm sure that would most definitely get me a slap.

"Of course you've got nothing to say. You need therapy or to get with this girl."

"I...I have..." I stammer like a fucking idiot.

"Have what?" Devney snaps, as though she's completely clueless.

"Been with her," I confess, biting my lip for a moment to think about my words, "But we've only kissed."

I don't want to tell Devney something private I shared with Ava, that I'll never fucking forget.

"Yeah well, I wish I'd never kissed you!" Devney shouts as she starts to storm out of my room.

I call out to her, "Devney, I'm sorry. Please come back to bed."

She turns to look back at me from my bedroom door.

"No, go fuck yourself, Zeke! Or go fuck her, because it's clear that's what you want."

She leaves then, slamming the door before I can say anything or stumble to my feet.

My thoughts wander to Ava and grabbing my phone I bring up FaceTime, dialling her even though I'm still naked from the waist down.

Seventeen

Ava

Lying on my bed, doing homework I'm startled when my iPad starts flashing with a FaceTime call.

I panic, seeing it's Zeke calling. We've hardly spoken to each other since the kiss at Dane's farewell.

In fact, he tried to talk to me, but I pushed him away.

To protect myself. And him.

Wicked Temptation

I wonder if I should answer it, or ignore it. My finger is hovering over reject but I'm worried something is wrong since it's getting late. He's never called or texted this late. And I also haven't heard from Ashton in a few days either.

So I answer sliding my finger over the accept button.

"Hey Z. Are you ok?"

He's smiling at me, so clearly nothing is wrong.

"Hey, Av's. And I'm ok...except for missing you," he tells me with a smirk.

I'm a little annoyed and my gaze drops from his face to his lack of underwear.

"Doesn't look like you're missing me, Ezekiel."

He laughs, irritating me more because he looks so damn sexy and I can't help but think about the last time I saw his dick.

"I always think of you when I wank, Av's. Do you think about me when you touch yourself Av's?" He asks, taunting me.

Sitting back on my bed, grabbing the iPad and resting it on my knees I try to meet his eyes on my screen.

"I don't touch myself," I stammer, annoyed that I can't even tell a little white lie to Zeke.

Again he laughs and I feel it everywhere—like he's touching me—even though he's not here.

"Oh really, Av's? I'm practically in your lap right now. Wanna touch yourself for me?"

"No...Zeke, what if Ashton hears you? Or my parents?"

"Come on Av's. I'm horny as fuck for you," he teases, his gaze dropping to my tits. "Those pj's are sexy too, baby."

I look down at my PJ top which is a plain white t-shirt.

"No, they're not."

Zeke laughs again and it makes me feel all tingly. I love his laugh.

"Av's I can see your nipples are hard through the fabric."

He's right, but he's not wearing underwear. It's like forbidden porn on my screen.

"You're wet for me, so play with me please, baby?" He asks with a seductive teasing smirk.

And god do I want to have FaceTime sex with him. To watch him touch himself whilst I do the same, but I can't.

"I can't Zeke. I have a boyfriend."

His eyes boggle at me, his mouth is agape. The denim blue of his eyes fades and he screeches out, "What?"

I nod, not able to look at him when I reply, "Yeah I'm seeing a guy from school. Drake Peters."

Zeke scoffs. "Seriously, you're with DP?"

"Yes. So please Ezekiel you...well this can't...happen anymore," I tell him, swallowing the lump in my throat.

"Have you fucked him?" He asks abruptly.

"No. But..." *I'm going to.* Even though I don't want to.

Zeke looks as heartbroken as I feel.

"Fine Av's I get it. I..." He hangs up, without finishing his last sentence leaving me feeling dumbfounded and upset...and horny.

I think about calling him back but even I know that's stupid.

Instead, I open up his Instagram. I start scrolling through a number of gorgeous pics of him, sliding my hand inside my PJ

Wicked Temptation

shorts to touch myself whilst ogling pics of him when I see a pic of him with a girl.

A really pretty girl who has her arm around him, and is kissing him on the cheek in another picture. It stabs at my heart.

I'm so upset.

I want to call him back and yell at him—to tell him that I hate him—but I don't think I could actually say the words out loud so I message him instead.

I hate you, Ezekiel. Looks like you have a girlfriend too.

Knew you liked me, Ava. Stalking me huh?

I don't like you. I hate you. Go fuck your girlfriend.

Don't have one. Devney is just a friend.

Whatever. Fuck you, Ezekiel.

Anytime you want Ava. Xx

I stifle a scream, throwing my iPad on the floor annoyed about his sexual innuendos and how much they affect me.

I hate myself.

I'm angry with myself for still having feelings for him when it's clear—even after our kiss at Dane's farewell—that he's moved on.

If he's moved on, then as much as it hurts I need to as well.

Eighteen

Ezekiel

Again I've been avoiding Devney like she's going to give me some STD just by looking at me, and I honestly feel like shit.

After a long day at uni, my head is pounding and I'm still thinking about the song I'm yet to write. The one that's a huge part of my final grade.

Ashton is nowhere to be found when I get home, so I quickly grab a beer from the fridge before heading up to my room, and sitting down on my bed, with the beer in my hand and my acoustic guitar on my lap.

I have my notebook open and after taking a guzzle of beer I put it down on my bedside table and grab a pen.

Only one person pops into my mind, as always.

Her
She loves me she hates me
I broke her heart But she broke mine first
Her
She hates me She loves me
I want her heart I want her all

It's not much, but it's a start and my mind is swimming with thoughts that I need to shut out again.

I finish the beer, deciding that I need to be drunk to finish the song. My black jeans, black t-shirt and leather jacket don't smell like B.O; even though I forgot to put on deodorant today in my haste to leave the house from sleeping in.

I really should get myself a damn car, but the thought of having a tram—as heavy as a rhino—up my arse whilst I'm trying to do a fucking hook turn scares the ever loving shit out of me.

Quickly, rushing into the bathroom I splash my fave cologne—Boss by Hugo Boss—on, and run a handful of gel through my hair, slicking it back a little.

And I grab my keys and phone, heading out the door and to the tram. It's only a ten minute trip to the club strip of High street and it's just on dusk when I walk into one of the pubs. There's some band playing and they're not bad.

I head up to the bar, ordering a whiskey when I spot her.

Devney is sitting at the other end of the bar with a couple of other chicks, drinking some cocktail that looks like melted fairy floss in a glass.

I don't want her to see me, but I also don't want to leave before I'm tanked. I down the first whiskey, signalling for another and a beer as well.

I gulp them both down, like they're water, and lean against the bar, scoping the dance floor for any talent other than Devney. She hasn't spoken to me since giving me a gobby, and I need to find another chick to get with, to get rid of the tension that's eating me alive.

I lock eyes with a brunette on the dance floor, who is grinding over her friends and staring at me.

It's fucking sexy, and I saunter over to her, grabbing her by the waist and pulling her against me. She murmurs and rocking to the music—dry humping her—without even thinking I kiss her. It's not mind blowing—hell, even Devney kisses better—but it's still hot and brownie is loving it.

The music changes, and breaking the kiss I step back from brownie, taking her in properly. She's grinning at me, like a cat who just devoured a whole bowl of cream. And I don't return the smile, because I'm quite frankly repulsed that I just kissed her. She's not ugly, but not exactly pretty, and I feel like chundering. I'm about to rush away to the dunnies when I feel someone step behind me, shoving a hand against my back.

I turn around to find Devney staring daggers at me.

"Seriously, Zeke!" she bellows, her hand up, dangerously close to my cheek.

"Hi duchess. What're you doing here?"

"I could ask you the same thing, arsehole."

Her hand still hasn't moved, and the fire in her eyes is really fucking intense.

I'm so getting bitch slapped.

"Needed a drink, duchess," I tell her with a smirk.

And that's when I feel it, her open palm slapping my cheek.

"You're an arsehole, Zeke!"

Clutching my throbbing cheek I chuckle, "Guilty, duchess. But you still want me."

"Aaahhh, fuck you, Zeke!" she bellows at me, storming towards the dunnies without looking back at me.

I don't wait around, as her friends trot after her, and I'm likely to get repeatedly bitch slapped if they set their sights on me, so even though I've been out for barely an hour I head home to drink myself into oblivion there instead.

I'll just have to wank away the tension still plaguing me instead.

Getting home I'm about to grab a beer and head up to my room when I pass the living room to see Ashton sculling a beer whilst pacing the room and cursing under his breath.

Stepping in the room, he stops pacing, and looks straight at me, almost through me. His stare is to blank. "Dude, you ok?" I ask, clicking my fingers in front of his face.

"No! I'm not fucking ok. Fuck!" he screams out, shaking his head violently.

"What Ash man?" I probe him, putting my hands on his shoulders to calm him down. "I'm here man, tell me what's going on."

He looks up at me with glassy eyes, like he's been crying. And my heart lurches in my chest. Something bad has happened to my best mate and I'm scared for him, hating seeing him on the precipice of losing his shit.

"He's dead," he blurts out suddenly.

"Who?" I ask pushing Ashton down so we're sitting on the couch. "Ash man, who's dead?"

He looks up at me, sniffing when he replies, "My dad."
Holy shitballs!

I was not expecting those words to spill out of his mouth.

"What man? How? Fuck."

Ashton takes a sip of his beer, gulping it down quickly when he replies with a melancholic tone, "Hung himself in his cell after another inmate beat him to a pulp."

"Shit, that's fucked up," I reply, letting his words sink in. "But at least you won't have to continue with the trial. I know that was weighing on you."

He nods at me.

"Yeah, like I'm happy. But I can't believe he's dead."

"Yeah, fucked up man. Way to sober up. I think we should go back out together and get shitfaced more."

"If it will make me forget then I'm down," he tells me, downing the last sips of his beer.

"Ripper man. Have you spoken to Tem?"

Wicked Temptation

"Yeah, called her before. She's shocked as well."

"Yeah, for sure. Fucked up definitely."

"Yep. Gonna head home on Monday to see her and help organise the funeral and shit. Not that he deserves one."

"Yeah, true man. Despite everything though, he was still ya dad. And it will give you some closure."

"Yeah, anyway let's go. Heard there's a sick band playing at Rock Off."

"Nice," I chant as we head out together.

Following Ashton to the tram, my thoughts wander to Ava again, wondering how she's feeling.

My fingers are itching to message her, but I hold back.

I don't want Ashton to see I'm messaging her and I'm also scared to see her again when we go home for the funeral, but I know I need to be there to support my second family, even if it will hurt like being stabbed in the heart.

Nineteen

Ezekiel

Standing in the Castello's living room after the funeral, I pull Ava against my side in a comforting hug. She hasn't stopped crying since we walked into the church, and my heart is fucking aching for her, breaking for her.

Fidel Castello was a cunt.

And didn't deserve Ava as his daughter but death—facing death—for any family member, no matter the circumstances rips your heart out. Ashton is with other family, and I feel kinda guilty that I'm comforting Ava and want to honestly comfort her by taking her upstairs, to kiss her and touch her—fuck her actually—until she forgets the pain she's feeling. But I can't do that.

I kiss the side of her head. "Av's, please don't cry, baby," I whisper. She looks up at me, turning in my embrace, and sobbing into my chest.

I pull her closer, hating that she's so upset—seeing her cry for her cunt of father—but also loving having her in my arms, no matter the circumstances.

She belongs with me.

I rest my chin on her head and let her cry, but she shifts back when he—her supposed fucking boyfriend—steps up to us.

I already feel empty without her in my arms. And I glare daggers at DP, taunting him like we're on the court. He was always a wuss player, never getting into the action and right now I'm towering over his weak arse, even though I'm probably only an inch taller than him.

He opens his mouth, and mutters, "I'm sorry about your Dad Ava." She nods at him and then looks to me.

I'm trying to get him to fuck off without words, but he's not getting the point. He has no idea about all the shit Ava has gone through with her father, and him trying to show he cares with a half-arsed I'm sorry is fucking laughable.

I pull her back against me, kissing the top of her head. "Thanks, DP. Av's appreciates it. But we need some time with our families now."

I glare at him again, my eyes darkening to tell him to rack off.

Ava turns in my embrace, and my heart skips a beat. I'm fucking loving that she's barely acknowledging him, and taking comfort in my arms.

The fucker is still standing there though, a sucker for punishment under my gaze. He honestly looks like he's about to take a leak in his pants. Ava looks up at me, brushing an arm across her cheeks, her sobbing finally subsiding.

"Thanks, Z. I...lo..."

Brushing a hand across her cheek I lean in closer, nearly kissing her again.

"Av's don't say things you don't mean."

She gulps, her eyes locked on mine, and god do I want to fucking kiss her to show her I love her too but I hold back because of Drake, who is staring at us as though I've stabbed him.

She turns to Drake, finding her voice, "Thanks for being here Drake. It means a lot."

And just like that she steps away from me and gives him a kiss. I see green or is it red? Who fucking cares? I'm pissed off, even though I shouldn't be.

"Ewww, Ava. Get a room, girl. This isn't the place for PDA's."

Breaking their kiss, Ava glares at me, her eyes stormy with anger at me. I know I'm an idiot, but seeing her kiss him; well I'd rather gauge my eyes out with scissors.

She stomps her foot. "Stop Ezekiel, please."

"Sorry, Av's but your boyfriend here is a bit of a tosser."

Wicked Temptation

Drake looks like he's going to cry. We'd taunted him on the basketball court with the name 'tosser' because he can't even toss a ball through the net when an inch away from it.

"You're an arsehole, Ezekiel! I don't know who you are right now. I might like you, as a friend but right now, you're starting to be an unsupportive jealous dickhead. And I hate you."

My heart hurts.

"Damn Av's. Stab me in the heart, baby."

"Fuck off! Or I will find Ashton and tell him you kissed me again."

Her eyes are betraying her. She wants to kiss me again. And even though DP is trying to stake his claim on her with an arm around her waist, Ava Castello is mine.

I don't say anything else but walk away leaving her in his arms for now.

My heart is broken, like a million fucking bullets have left holes in it.

Twenty

Ava

S tupidly I'm still nervous—in a nauseous way—to be out on a date with Drake. It's our third date, and I should be enjoying his company but someone else is on my mind.

I know I shouldn't be thinking about him, especially when he was an arsehole at Dad's funeral but Ezekiel Alessio is tattooed on my heart.

"Ava sit down yeah? You're making me nervous," Drake says from below me.

He's sitting on the picnic blanket he's laid out on the grass under a huge shady gumtree in Beachview park. Being here, so close to the basketball court reminds me of days playing basketball with my brother and Zeke, and I choke on the deep breath I swallow as I sit down.

Drake pats my back.

"Breathe. Ava." He's glaring at me. And I feel so uncomfortable.

"Sorry, I'm ok. I ahh, just um…"

"What's wrong? Are you cold?"

"No, I um…was thinking about Zeke."

"Oh, well. Um. Shit," Drake says, not meeting my eyes. "He was acting all weird at the funeral. Is something going on with you guys?"

I shake my head, biting down on my lip and muttering, "No, it's nothing like that. He was just being protective because he's known me my whole life."

"Oh right. It kinda seemed like more to me, Ava."

He looks so sad, and I hate that I'm about to lie to him.

"It's not. He's like a brother to me." Drake isn't convinced but he shrugs it off. "This is really sweet by the way."

"Thanks, I did it for you. I've been planning this date for weeks, before the funeral. But I nearly cancelled because of Zeke." His tone is so sad.

I don't like seeing him hurt by Zeke's intimidation and bullying.

"I'm sorry that you felt intimidated by Zeke. I promise there is nothing going on between us."

I touch his knee, and a smile curves the corner of his lips.

"Fine if you say so, Ava. But honestly, I really like you."

"I like you to," I tell him, swallowing down the lump in my throat that those words cause.

"Show me," he teases, leaning closer to me.

He kisses me, and lazily kissing him back we lie down on the picnic blanket. His hands slide up under my dress, grazing the elastic of my knickers a moment before he shimmies them up to my side, closer to my boobs.

I can feel his dick hardening and pressing against me through the lace of my knickers. It feels good.

His touch doesn't have the same effect on me as Zeke's but it's still good.

I murmur against his lips, teasing him a little with my tongue before pulling back to ask him, "Are you a virgin, Drake?"

He nods, frowning at me as though he's ashamed. "Yeah. Are you?"

"Yeah," I mutter, regretting asking the question.

"We could. You know. If you want. No pressure."

"Yeah maybe. But not here," I reply with a laugh, which Drake follows by laughing too and sitting up a little.

"Of course not," he says with a smirk. "And not yet. I should probably take you on another date first."

"Yeah. Isn't the rule five dates?"

He laughs again, nervously. "I don't know. I've never had a girlfriend before."

Wicked Temptation

"Yeah. I've never had a boyfriend either," I confess.

"Until now?" Drake says like a question.

"Yeah," I reply, kissing him again.

We kiss for a bit, and I tell myself to let go. To just feel, and not think about how Zeke, and his touch makes me feel alive but Drake's doesn't even give me tingles.

Sleeping with Drake is probably going to be a bad decision but pining after Zeke and thinking about sleeping with him instead of my boyfriend is stupid.

My thoughts as I'm kissing Drake are just a muddle and I pull back from the kiss shivering.

"You cold?"

"Yeah, we should probably head home before it gets dark."

"Yeah, it's getting cold," he says standing up and taking my hand to help me up.

Quickly we pack up our picnic stuff and head back to his car holding hands.

The only thing I can think of is that I wish this date, and this moment holding hands was with Ezekiel. I've got it so bad for the boy—man—I can't have.

Twenty-One

Ezekiel

Despite my argument—and getting bitch slapped—I've actually been speaking to Devney, which is good since we've been put into a small group for an assignment. It's some lame thing about comparing musicians of the past to a current musician of the same genre. I have no clue what to even do, and all I can think of is seeing Ava strutting around in her old band t-shirts and nothing else.

Devney is sitting across from me, and the table in front of us is strewn with books. The other group members are beside

Wicked Temptation

her and she keeps sniggering about something with one of our classmates and looking up at me. It's making me feel uncomfortable and out of the loop. Every time I try to say something to her she abruptly shuts me down.

I need to get her away from the rest of our group, so when they pack and leave, I step up behind Devney's chair and lean down to whisper in her ear, "Devney, please can we talk?" I nearly call her 'duchess' but I know she hates it and she'd probably shove me away again and I really do need to talk to her.

She turns to face me and I rest my arse on the edge of the table.

"What about Zeke?" she asks with a hint of cheekiness in her voice.

Giving her a smirk, I reply, "Us."

"You told me there isn't an us," she chastises me. "And can't be an us."

I sigh. "I know. And I should explain why."

She fiddles with the books on the table.

"Fine," she snaps, looking up at me. "Tell me why you're such an arsehole then."

Again I sigh, taking in a deep breath that I exhale when I reply, "Well as you know I'm in love with a girl back home." My heart is pounding in my chest, just thinking of Ava and my next words hurt. "But I can't be with her."

"Yeah, sucks, why?"

"She's my best mate's little sister. And he practically beats me up every time I even look at her." I'm frowning and Devney is giving me an odd look like she actually cares.

"Oh...That really sucks," she says abruptly, before continuing with a smirk on her face. "But sounds like you need to move on."

"I know Devney." I'm practically seething through my teeth. "But I can't. And I'm sorry I've hurt you in the process." This convo is not going the way I'd planned. I should've just let it be, but I'm a sucker for punishment, clearly.

"Yeah, well, I really like you, Zeke. But I can't keep putting myself out there if you're not going to return my feelings."

"I get that. And I'm really sorry," I tell her shaking my head before asking, "Can we at least be friends?"

It's a long shot, but I haven't really made any other friends in my classes thus far. I'm not shy, but I haven't put myself out there much.

I don't need others in my life who won't give a shit about me when things go south.

"Yeah, I guess. And um..." I'm intrigued about what's she's thinking. I feel like something is going to happen and I steady myself on the table with my palms.

"What Dev?" I jeer, making her look at me oddly. I instantly regret the new nickname. But she doesn't seem to notice and doesn't react like she does when I call her duchess.

"Well, if we're just friends, do you think your best mate would mind if I crash with you guys for a bit?"

I think about her question a moment. It's a bad idea, but having her living with us might make it easier to move on.

"Nah why? What's going on?" I query.

Wicked Temptation

"My roomie's boyfriend is an abusive douche and I can't stand listening to their rough daddy kink sex anymore," she tells me in one quick sentence in a monotone voice.

"Oh shit," I reply loudly, trying not to gag. "Yeah, bring ya stuff over tonight. Ash will deal."

I grab a piece of paper and scribble my address on it, handing it to her when she replies, "Thanks, Zeke. Maybe you're not an arsehole after all."

She gives me a sweet smile. And stands up to pull me into a hug. It feels platonic, just two friends—now roommates—hugging.

We quickly finish packing up our things, and she sashays out winking at me at the door. "See you later tonight, roomie!" she jeers.

I don't reply, instead, I grab my bag and head out, googling on my phone where the closest basketball court is.

I need to let off some steam.

Twenty-Two

Ezekiel

It's been a week since Devney moved in. Most of the time I've hardly seen her as she's kept to herself, except for the awkward moment when she forgot to knock and barged on me—in the bathroom—whilst I was wrapping one of our black towels around my waist. She was all apologetic and i threw the towel at her head, walking out starkers. Turning back to look at her she sniffed the towel like a creeper and I had to laugh, because even though I said I wouldn't I'd wiped my jizz on the black towel after my shower wank session thinking of Ava.

And I'm honestly pissed with Dev. She's deliberately teasing me, flitting around the house in practically nothing. Her go to outfit is boy short knickers and tank tops, that show off her tits. And I can't help but stare. It makes me feel like a damn cheater, but I do have to admit I'm attracted to Devney.

I keep pushing her away because my heart belongs to Ava, and I want my body to belong to my Ava as well but fuck me dead I need sex.

Heading into the kitchen for some grub after coming home from shooting some hoops at the local park, I'm sweaty, and wipe my face with my white t-shirt.

"Fuck, um…" I hear Devney come into the room behind me. She's in an oversized t-shirt that shows off the curve of her arse, and the fact she's only wearing a g-string. She licks her lips, watching me as she saunters into the kitchen.

"Dev, please do you mind?"

"What, Zeke?" she teases, fluttering her fucking eyelashes at me, and leaning on the bench, jutting her hip out seductively.

Fuck, I'm horny.

This little display is making Z-man have a damn party.

Pointing at her I taunt, "I can't have you flitting around the house wearing nothing."

"I'm not naked Zeke."

"Yeah but you're not wearing much Dev. And I'm a guy."

My eyes gaze over her body again, and it's clear she's not wearing a bra.

"Don't be a dick, Zeke."

"Wasn't trying to be," I jeer, smirking at her, and stepping a little closer to her towards the fridge.

"Sure you weren't," she teases stepping closer to me. I turn to the fridge to get a drink out and when I turn back around she's right behind me and our bodies collide; accidentally caging her against the counter.

She takes a deep breath in, staring at me. And without thinking, I kiss her hard. She kisses me back, licking my lips for entrance and murmuring into my mouth, pushing her body against my dick.

God, it feels good, but fuck no...what am I fucking doing?

Abruptly I break the kiss, stepping back and screwing the lid off the bottle of water I'm practically crushing in my fist.

"Shit, I'm sorry. I shouldn't have done that."

Devney is just smirking at me, not saying a word when I rush out of the kitchen, bounding up the stairs to the bathroom.

I'm so fucking angry with himself. I might be fucking horny, but I shouldn't be kissing Devney.

Stripping from my basketball shorts and t-shirt I turn the shower on, thankful it takes a minute to warm up. Standing under the spray of water, I let it wash over me, cursing myself for my stupid actions.

It feels like I've just cheated on Ava. And that's fucking stupid.

Ava is not my girlfriend. She can't be my girlfriend and I shouldn't be thinking about her—wanting her—when I could just get out of my own damn head and fuck Devney.

Wicked Temptation

But I don't want Devney.

Quite frankly, I want to forget that last kiss happened because now I don't think I'll be able to stop myself from going further if anything else happens with Devney.

Getting out of the shower, I pull my basketball shorts back on after drying off with my jizz stained towel and head to my bedroom.

Flopping down on my bed I stare at my phone in my hand. I know I shouldn't, but I can't help myself. I need to see her.

Connecting FaceTime I wait, not expecting her to pick up because we've hardly spoken to each other this past month since the funeral. But she does and I smile, greeting her, "Hey Av's," when her gorgeous happy face appears on my screen.

"Hey Z. What's up?" she says happily, holding her phone up as she starts to move towards her bedroom door.

"Nothing. Just miss you," I admit, with a cocky smirk. "And damn Av's you look gorgeous."

"Um yeah, thanks," she mutters. "I'm going out with Drake. Our fifth date."

"Oh...Things are getting serious then?" I ask, swallowing the lump in my throat. She's moving on.

"Yeah, I like him a lot," she tells me, her tone sad. "And Zeke I really have to go. Say hello to Ash for me."

She hangs up. And I laugh to myself, thinking, *'yeah right.'* Ashton doesn't even know how much I've been talking to her, how much I think about her. And he has no idea that I'm hopelessly in love with her.

It hurts but I know exactly why Ava was looking so sexy. The fifth date most likely means she's going to sleep with him. And that makes me angry and insanely fucking jealous.

I want her to share that with me. But I know I shouldn't be thinking that way.

I was lucky enough to give her her first kiss. And that's all I deserve.

Ava is to good for me.

I'll only break her, ruin her when everything comes crashing down.

Twenty-Three
Ava

After the date, we go back to Drake's house. His parents are at work—night shift—and he takes my hand leading me down a long hallway to his room.

He closes the door, even though no one is home. And that makes me feel more nervous than I already am. I know what's going to happen and I want to, but I don't.

Drake is staring at me, a wicked smile on his face, but he speaks softly, "You look so pretty, Ava. Are you sure you still wanna do it?"

"Yeah, I'm sure," I tell him, kissing him and stumbling back towards his bed by the window. We fall against it, still kissing. He breaks it, pulling his t-shirt over his head. He's got muscles, but he's a little scrawny; compared to Zeke that is. My heart pounds and my clit throbs when thoughts of Zeke come to mind. I shouldn't be thinking of Ezekiel when I'm about to have sex—for the first time—with someone else, but thinking of him is the only way I'm going to even be able to go through with this.

I know that's stupid, and probably really hurtful to Drake. But being with him doesn't turn me on the way being with Zeke does.

Gulping I stand up, and Drake laughs, kissing me again. His hands reach up under my dress, teasing the waistband of my leggings that he yanks down without warning. I'm not wearing knickers and he murmurs against my lips when his fingers brush over my bare skin.

I can feel his hardening dick pressing against me through his jeans. And reaching between us I fumble with his belt and fly, yanking his jeans down to show his black y-front jocks. He sits up, pulling his jeans off and grabbing a condom from his back pocket before he throws them on the floor.

He shoves his jocks down to, and he's completely naked—vulnerable—and hard. I'm still wearing my bra and I feel like I'm naked.

Wicked Temptation

Rolling the condom down over his erection, he glares at me. It stirs up nausea in my stomach again.

"Are you sure, Ava?" Drake asks me again, his dick rubbing against my bare crotch.

"I'm sure, Drake," I gulp, as he leans over my body to kiss me as he slips inside me.

His thrusts are slow at first, letting me adjust to the feeling and I hiss at the pain when he breaks the barrier that signals my descent into womanhood. I bite down on my lip to stifle the screams I want to let out; both pain and a hint of pleasure.

"Ava, are you ok?" Drake asks, concern in his tone. He stills inside me.

"Yeah, it just hurt a bit. Keep going," I tell him with a smile.

Drake starts rocking in and out of my body, my name on his lips, but I'm not thinking about him.

I'm thinking about Zeke the whole time, closing my eyes and pretending it's him to block out the hurt.

I'm broken from my dirty fantasy, stilling the rocking of my hips to meet the thrusts of his dick inside me by his hoarse voice, "Fuck, Ava! I'm going to come."

I feel Drake's dick throb inside me as he climaxes, filling the condom inside me before he pulls out.

I didn't come.

It felt good, but the hurt outweighed the pleasure until I thought of Zeke.

Drake lays down beside me, pulling me against his side a moment and kissing me softly.

"That was so good, huh?"

"Yeah, really good," I lie, biting down on my lip before I say something else that isn't a lie.

"Stay the night with me Av's?" He asks, using my nickname. I don't like hearing it on his lips, and the tears start to fall down my cheeks.

I don't want this. I've just made the biggest mistake of my life.

Sheer panic, regret is thrumming through my body and I jump up off the bed like it's on fire. "Um, Drake, I'm sorry. I have to get home. My mum doesn't have a key and my stepdad is out of town. I have to go."

I pick up my clothes, pulling my dress back on so quickly and rushing out that Drake doesn't even get to reply before I'm out the door and running home in tears.

Running into the house, I kick my shoes off at the front door and I find mum in the kitchen; making a hot chocolate.

I let out a sigh, wondering if I should ignore mum's caring stare and run upstairs to cry into my pillow. She sips her hot chocolate and asks me softly, "Ava dear, what's wrong?"

I look at her and down at the breakfast bar stools. I want to run away, but also run into her arms and cry.

"I...mum...I..." I mutter, not sure if I'm ready to share my monumental fuck up with mum.

She's always been so open with us—about everything in life—about sex.

She'd had the birds and bees convo with me when I was twelve after Dane's twenty first birthday party, and I'd noticed Zeke staring at me with a bulge in the front of his board shorts.

Wicked Temptation

I'd pretty much been crushing on Zeke since then, but my feelings only deepened as I got older and when we kissed at my sixteenth birthday.

"What dear?" Mum questions, motioning towards the stools. "Sit down. I'll make you a hot choccie."

The tears are still stinging my eyes when I sit down on the breakfast bar stool, kicking my feet against the base board.

Mum's back is turned, and she starts to make my hot chocolate, when I blurt out, "I did something stupid mum."

She turns back around, again asking, "What dear? You can talk to me."

Sighing again, I take in a deep breath to calm myself. I honestly can't believe I'm about to tell my mum about losing my virginity.

"I had sex with Drake," I say softly, again exhaling a breath before continuing, "And I shouldn't have mum. It hurt so much."

"Oh dear, hun," Mum replies with a caring tone. "Were you safe?" she asks. *Definitely thinking like a mother.*

"Yes, but I shouldn't have done it," I tell her, sniffing back the tears still stinging my eyes. "I didn't want my first time to be with him."

"Oh dear, what do you mean?" Mum asks, her eyes and expression showing concern. "You're friends and you've been seeing him for a while now."

"Well yes...but I...wanted to lose my virginity to someone I love and I..." I can't get the rest of the words out, breaking down into tears.

Mum comes around to my side of the bench, pulling me into a hug. And whispering softly against my hair, "Oh Ava. It's ok. You don't have to tell me, hun."

She rubs my hair then, soothing me before kissing my forehead. "I know dear, I know," she says softly.

I pull back from the hug, looking at her confused.

"You know?"

"Know what, Ava?" Mum asks back, giving me the same confused look.

"That I...love..." I cut my words off, gulping, wanting to hear what I'm thinking from mum instead to make sure she's thinking the same thing.

"That you love Ezekiel," she says with no real emotion in her tone.

"Yeah, how'd you know?" I ask, scared she's going to tell me something I don't want to hear.

She lets out a slight laugh.

"I've seen how you looked at him all these years, Ava. And I know about Ashton hitting him at our wedding because he kissed you."

I swear I blush, thinking about what else happened between Zeke and I after her wedding.

"I'm sorry mum. I know I shouldn't love him, but I do."

Mum nods, smiling at me.

"You can't help who you love, dear. But I want you to be careful with your heart," she tells me, kissing my forehead again. "And your body to. I trust you."

"Thanks, mum, I love you," I tell her grabbing the hot chocolate from the bench as I slide off the stool. "Goodnight."

Wicked Temptation

"Goodnight dear," she replies softly, again kissing my forehead before I head out of the kitchen.

Once In my bedroom, I sit on my bed. And grab my phone to send Zeke a text. I know I shouldn't be still talking to him—sending him messages—but I can't help it. He's always on mymind, and he's practically tattooed on my heart.

I miss you. I want to see you.

I'm not expecting a reply, so taking a sip of my hot chocolate I'm surprised when my phone buzzes on the bed next to me. My heart swells seeing his name on my phone.

Opening the message I want to cry all over again. His words both make my heart pound and break at the same time.

Miss you to, Ava. So much. But you have a boyfriend.

And you have a girlfriend.

No Ava. Dev is not my girlfriend. I don't want her.

I don't want my boyfriend either.

What? Did something happen?

I don't reply after that. I can't tell Zeke I lost my virginity. He'd either not care or make a joke of it, and make me feel even worse than I already do.

I like Drake, but I don't love him. And I'm regretting my choice to sleep with him, especially when I stand up to get into my pj's and blood has trickled down my thighs.

Drake didn't even care about my feelings, that he tore me apart.

I know Ezekiel would've let me finish and would've cared for me. I'm such an idiot.

I don't want Drake.

If I can't have Ezekiel Alessio, I don't want anyone.

Twenty-Four

Ezekiel

Ava doesn't reply to my last text about what's happened with her and D P. And it has me a little scared, but also I'm intrigued and I miss her so damn much.

A sudden—albeit crazy—idea pops into my head, and throwing my phone down on my bed I barge out of my room to Ashton's room.

I can hear some odd noises, a moaning scream like sound but without knocking I push the door open to find my best mate with his daks down; FaceTiming with Tem.

Caz May

He quickly yanks up his boxers as I cross the room to his bed.

It's awkward as fuck.

I practically saw my best mate's hard dick. And I have to fight back the urge to chunder all over him when I tease, "Shit man, I thought you were dying or something."

Ashton glares at me, not replying even when I look to the iPad screen on the pillow on his knees.

Tempany is on the screen, wearing some sexy nightie.

"Oh hey Tem," I jeer, giving her a wink. "Sexy outfit but since you're speaking to Ash here I had an idea."

I look back to my best mate, who is still giving me dagger eyes. "What's that dickwad?"

A smile spreads across my face when I reply, "That Tem and Av's come to visit in the July holidays."

Ashton glares at me a moment and then looks back to Tem on his screen.

"Baby, what you think?" he asks her with a smile that he'd only give her.

"Sounds great," she replies eagerly. "I can speak to Ava, but I'm sure she'll be all for it. She misses you."

I gulp, clutching my chest to stifle my laugh.

"Ripper," I jeer, nodding to Tem on the screen. "I'm going to leave you two to get back to your dirty business. And we'll work out details later."

Neither of them reply as I leave the room. Ashton's eyes follow me out and I pretend to wank and vomit at the same time, laughing when he gives me an up yours and I close the door behind me.

Wicked Temptation

My mind is racing and I'm not exactly looking where I'm going as I head to the kitchen, so it's no surprise when I bump into Devney coming out of the bathroom. My eyes scan her, and I grunt in frustration. She's only in a towel, her long blonde locks damp and clinging to her wet skin.

"Dev, I thought I told you to wear more clothes," I tease, giving her a smirk.

"You did," she jeers with a smirk as well. "But I forgot to take clothes into the bathroom."

"Right," I reply sarcastically, still not able to get the smile off my face.

"What's got you so excited?" She asks, with a suggestive wink, looking at the front of my trackies to see if my excitement is related to her being in a towel. I laugh at her.

"Put a dirty plan into action to see my girl in a month or so."

"Ooo...nice. Can't wait to meet her," she replies, her eyes flashing with some odd emotion that seems like jealousy to me.

She runs off towards her room, and I slap her arse playfully, before jumping on the edge of the balustrade and sliding down on my arse to head to the kitchen.

I need a damn beer to get my mind to go numb, or I'm going to be thinking about doing the dirty with Ava—and Devney—all night long.

Caz May

Twenty-Five

Ava

Since the night Drake and I slept together I've been avoiding him.

Part of me is glad to no longer be a virgin, but part of me also regrets it. It's not as though I would ever have the chance

Wicked Temptation

to sleep with Zeke, so at least now I'm not holding on to my v-card for the guy I'll never have.

Drake has tried to speak to me at school and has sent me countless messages. It's clear he's distraught that I'm pushing him away.

He confronts me at lunch, a week later. I want to walk away, but he's cornered me at one of the bleachers near our other friends. They must see that things have been weird between us.

"Ava please can we talk?"

"I...um...ok," I stammer walking off to the other side of the bleachers with him following me. I don't want our friends to hear this conversation.

I lean against the bleachers, folding my arms across my chest defensively whilst glaring at him. I don't know what to say. I have no words to start this inevitable conversation—that we should've had after we had sex—not a week later.

"Why haven't you talked to me since we, you know?"

For fucks sake, he can't even say it.

"Because I shouldn't have slept with you Drake," I blurt out, rather calmly.

"Why Ava? I thought you liked me."

"I do like you Drake. But I'm not in love with you," I tell him, feeling a weight lift off my shoulders. But my gut still aches when I say, "And I regret us."

He takes a step back from me, and I can finally breathe, but his words are sad and angry.

"Oh, fuck Ava. That hurts."

"I'm sorry. I can't change how I feel."

"Fine...so are we breaking up then?"

I nod, trying to look at him, even though he's looking at the ground.

"Yeah. I'm sorry Drake. I really am. You're a great guy, just not the guy for me."

He looks up, a smile curving his lips that he can't help.

"Well, Ava, I'm really hurt, but I don't want you to be unhappy. So maybe we could be friends?"

"Yeah, I'd like that," I reply, pulling him into a hug.

It could feel weird, but it doesn't. It's a friendly hug like we'd shared before we kissed and slept together. And I'm happy about that, even if my heart is hurting for him. I head back to the other end of the bleachers where Dakota is with our other friends chatting.

She gives me a friendly smile, handing me an iced coffee.

"Everything ok, A?" my best friend asks with a frown.

"Yeah, Kota, I'm ok. But Drake and I just broke up."

"Oh, are you sure you're ok?" she asks innocently. She knows I'm not really into Drake, but she doesn't know I lost my virginity to him. She'd probably keel over if I told her that.

"Yeah. It was my choice. I can't love him."

My sweet bestie laughs then, asking, "Still love Zeke?"

"Yeah," I reply, sipping my iced coffee a moment. "And Tempany said we're going to visit the boys in the holidays so I'm excited about seeing him," I tell my best friend, a smile lighting up my face from thinking about Zeke.

Dakota giggles.

"Ooo...are you going to tell him how you feel about him?"

Wicked Temptation

I shrug. "I don't know. Might be difficult with my brother around, but I'll see."

Again Dakota giggles, and I smile at her when the bell goes and we head to class.

Twenty-Six
Ava

H aphazardly I'm shoving clothes from my open drawers and wardrobe into my pink Adidas gym bag.

It's been a bitterly cold start to winter and packing to go to the boys, I don't know what to take for the week. I'm throwing

Wicked Temptation

in all sorts of things in the bag—dresses, my band t-shirts, a bikini and sexy underwear—when Tem comes in.

"Hey, Ava, how's the packing going?" she asks smiling at me. She has a small suitcase on wheels at her feet.

"Horrible," I grunt, shoving some socks into the side pocket of my bag.

"Why's that?" Tem asks, coming further into my room, and sitting on my bed next to my bag.

"I have no idea what to pack. What we're going to be doing and stuff."

"Makes sense. But it's Melbourne so even though it's winter you need all seasonal clothes."

"I know. That's so frustrating," I reply exasperated, putting my thongs and converse in as well as a strappy pair of black heels that I can barely walk in.

I've packed my sequinned little black dress—that barely covers my underwear—and I hope there will be a time to wear it. It's one of my favourites as it shows off my cleavage dipping into a v at the front. I want to wear it to see if Zeke still looks at me as though he has the hots for me.

Just thinking about Zeke's gaze on me in the dress—and the other outfits I've packed—is making my heart race. I can't help but smile.

"Are you excited?" Tem asks, seeing my smile as I zip up the bag.

"Yeah, I can't wait to see Zeke again," I tell my stepsister, who sniggers at me for forgetting to mention my brother too, so I add, "And Ashton to of course."

"Yeah, I can't wait to see Ash. I've missed being with him so much."

"Yeah, you've definitely been moping around."

She laughs. "I know, but phone sex isn't the same."

"Eww, Tem. Don't tell me about you having sex with my brother." I pretend to gag. And she laughs before asking with a smirk, "Speaking of Ashton, are you going to tell him how you feel about Zeke?"

"I cant. He'll kill Zeke if he touches me, again."

Tem gives me a sweet smile. I'm practically about to cry. Confessing to my big brother I'm in love with his best friend needs to happen, but I can't tell him.

I can't lose Ezekiel completely. He's a part of me.

It's always been him who's had my heart. And the last months have only confirmed that I'm probably going to be alone forever because no one else will ever own my heart.

Ezekiel Alessio has ruined me for anyone else. And I've only kissed him and come apart with him once. But even so, he's the only one to make me feel alive. And I'm going to do something about it these holidays.

It seems Tempany agrees as she softly says, "You can't keep hiding how you feel, Av's."

"I know. But what if he really doesn't feel the same way?"

Again Tem laughs, but it's sweet. "Are you really asking that?"

"Yeah, I...um..." I have no idea what I'm saying.

"I've seen the way Zeke looks at you Ava. I think he's hiding how he feels about you because of Ashton."

Wicked Temptation

"Yeah, maybe," I mutter picking up my bag to sling it over my shoulder.

"And it's about time your brother realises how his anger towards you guys being together is making you both sad."

"Yeah, definitely. Are you ready to go?"

"Yeah, definitely ready," she replies standing up and grabbing her suitcase to wheel it out behind her as we head downstairs to her car.

Putting our bags in the backseat, we get in and head to the city.

I crank up the music and her tiny Fiat pumps with the beat of songs that make me think of Zeke, and telling him I'm in love with him.

I'm going to kiss him again, and hopefully do a lot more than just kiss him if I can get just a moment alone with him.

Twenty-Seven

Ezekiel

I'm antsy, walking around the apartment on tenterhooks. Inviting the girls to stay for a week was a stupid idea.

I'm pacing the room, waiting for the sound of Tempany's little Fiat grunting as she pulls up to the curb.

Ashton is glaring at me, scoffing under his breath.

"Dude, calm ya tits. Anyone would think the damn queen is visiting."

I laugh at him, trying to calm my nerves and think of something to say that isn't going to be a bumbling confession of my feelings for Ava.

"Your queen is coming dufus. Thanks to me."

"Yeah my temptress is coming, so why're you acting like a lunatic?"

"No reason. Just want them both here safe for you."

He gives me a side eye look, his eyebrows raising up as though he's about to say some smartarse comment.

"Yeah right, dickwad. Keep ya dick in ya grey trackies."

I'm about to reply when the girls arrive, Tempany's car screeching to a halt in the street outside.

I want to run outside and squeeze Ava into a hug, to crush her sexy body against mine and feel her tits pressed against my chest.

Z-man is practically about to burst out of my trackies at the mere thought of having her that close again.

But this situation is awkward enough without me being a damn creeper on my best mate's little sister when he's being so weird about the girls visiting.

I'd convinced him by telling him it was for him to see Tempany—without the prying eyes of his parents—but that was a big fat lie.

My reason was purely selfish; to see Ava and hopefully make her mine this time.

Opening the front door, I watch the girls walking up the path.

My eyes can't look away from Ava.

Caz May

She looks absolutely gorgeous, wearing boyish black three striped adidas trackies and an oversized band t-shirt with 'The Killers' on it. I snigger at her loving them, and the reference to her being a killer of my damn heart. Her blonde hair is down, falling in waves over her shoulders and she's clutching the strap of pink gym bag as though it's a prized possession and holds all her secrets. I think about all the cute—sexy—outfits and underwear she's got hiding in there, but honestly the only outfit I really want to see her in right now is her birthday suit.

When the girls reach the door Ashton is being an arse. He doesn't even greet Ava at all, completely brushing off his little sister to focus his attention on Tempany.

I get it, he's missed his girlfriend, but no doubt Ava has missed her big brother as well. And with all the shit that went down with their dad—his death and funeral—the least he could do is show some happiness at having her here.

He wraps Tempany in his arms, murmuring something incoherent into her ear that makes her giggle as they fuck off to his room, bounding up the stairs so quick they're practically a blur.

Not that I honestly give a damn shit, because their absence means I get to spend time with Av's alone.

She drops her bag, and glares at me. Tears are stinging her eyes, and it cuts me deep. Without thinking I pull her against me in a hug, inhaling the sweet vanilla scent of her hair.

Fuck, she smells good. The vanilla scent of her hair, and the intoxicating perfume that is clearly gardenia's like mum loves to grow in her garden back home. I murmur against Ava's hair. "Hey Av's."

Wicked Temptation

She steps back, and my arms feel so fucking empty, but the smile on her face hits me in the feels. "Hi Z."

I'm tongue tied. All I can do is stare at her, completely fucking mesmerised by her and overwhelmed, not quite believing she's here, in my damn house.

I pick up her bag with a smile, and she follows me up the stairs to the guest room next to Devney's.

Opening the door, she walks in looking around when I put her bag on the bed. "I'll leave you to get settled in. I'll be in the kitchen if you need me."

I want to kiss her. I don't want to walk out of the room, but push her down on the bed and kiss her until we both can't take it a second longer but I can't.

"Thanks, Z," she replies with a smile as I walk out to leave her for a bit.

I head back downstairs to the kitchen to get a drink, to hopefully distract myself from thoughts of racing upstairs and kissing Ava until my lips hurt; until Z-man is so painfully hard that I make her mine.

Devney is in the kitchen, holding a beer in her hands. She waves it at me, when she taunts, "You got it bad for her, huh?"

I gulp, wondering how long she'd been standing in the kitchen watching me with Ava.

"Might. But can't go there Dev. She's my best mate's little sister."

"So," she replies, with a hint of laughter that doesn't meet her eyes. "If you love her you should..." I don't let her complete the sentence.

"I said I can't Dev ok. He'll kill me."

Again she laughs, with a bit more malice.

"Suit yourself, Zeke. If you want to forget her you know where my bedroom is."

She walks off, heading upstairs. I get a drink out of the fridge and gulp it down without tasting it.

I know I should leave her alone, but I can't so I head back upstairs, straight to the guest—Ava's—room. The door is closed so I knock against it with a fist and barely a minute passes before she opens it to me.

I gasp, completely breathless.

Ava Castello takes my breath away.

Wicked Temptation

Twenty-Eight
Ava

*O*pening the bedroom door to Zeke, his gaze wanders my body, even though my outfit isn't anything special. I've kept my trackies on but changed my top to a midriff baring long-sleeved crop top and cardigan that brushes against my bare hips. It shows off my belly button ring.

Caz May

Zeke clearly likes the outfit change, his denim eyes darkening. And he's breathless, shocked, gasping and taking a deep breath in when he asks, "Hey Av's. You ok?"

"Yeah. Why?" I ask, curious as to why he would think I'm anything but fine.

Yes, my own brother dismissed my arrival without a second thought, but I get it that he's missed Tempany.

They're so in love, it's sickening.

It's not like I can talk when I'm just as in love with the gorgeous guy standing in front of me.

"Ripper, so um...wanna get out of here for a bit?" A smirk appears on his face, and it makes my stomach flip.

"But Ashton will find out," I blurt out, stepping closer to Zeke.

He laughs, with a wicked smirk. "He's busy Av's. I don't think him and Tem will be coming out of his room before midnight."

I laugh in response, clutching my stomach and pretending to vomit. "Eww Z, I don't need to hear that."

"Sorry," he mutters, stepping out of the door jamb. "But truth Av's."

I don't reply, just nod and smile when he takes my hand, and my whole body tingles, goosebumps erupting all over my skin.

"Come on...let's go. I wanna take you somewhere."

Blindly I follow him downstairs, and out the front door.

As we run down the street his hand is still in mine, his grip tight and his fingers interlaced with mine.

Wicked Temptation

I can't stop smiling.

This feels so real like Ezekiel is mine.

Mine to love.

Reaching the main street he drags me onto the tram that pulls up when he hails it to a stop.

We sit down, and he drops my hand. My heart lurches, missing the contact of his hand in mine. But his eyes are still on me, staring at me like he still can't believe I'm sitting next to him.

I giggle softly, running a hand along his thigh, over the fabric of his grey trackies.

"Why are you staring at me Z?" I ask in a teasing tone.

He chuckles, his whole body vibrating. It's fucking sexy.

"Cause you're stunning Av's," he tells me with a sexy wink.

I'm fucking tongue tied and feel hot all over at what his words imply. "You know that. And I can't believe you're here."

"You're pretty sexy yourself," I say with a laugh.

His whole face lights up, his eyes sparkling like a crystal blue lake when the sun catches it.

I love his eyes so much, especially when he's looking at me like I'm the only girl in the room.

The only girl in his world.

"So where are we going?" I query with a teasing tone when he doesn't reply.

He chuckles again, his hand gripping mine that's still resting on his thigh.

"Not telling," he teases, again with his sexy smirk.

Wherever we're going I'm possibly not going to make it there because I'm about to be a puddle at his feet. That smirk directed at me makes me want to melt.

"Fine. Tease."

"You love me," he teases, winking at me.

I gulp, not replying because I'm not sure what to say to that.

My heart is telling me to say, *'yeah I do love you,'* but my head is like *'shut your damn trap Ava, he didn't mean it that way.'*

Standing up when the tram stops he takes my hand again —lacing our fingers together—as we run along a busy street to our destination.

Twenty-Nine

Ezekiel

Ava is glaring at me, then looking at the tattoo shop in front of us that we've abruptly stopped at.

"Z, what are we doing here?"

"I'm getting a tatt, Av's. I've been thinking about it for months."

"Oh um, cool. What're you gonna get?"

"Come in and find out," I jeer at her, dragging her inside. She glances around, not letting go of my hand even when I step up to the front desk.

Caz May

I speak to the guy behind the counter and quickly decide on what I'm getting when Ava suddenly speaks, "Do you do piercings as well?"

"Yeah, sweets. What you after?"

"My tongue," she declares, sassy and rebellious. And damn, it turns me on. I practically grunt thinking about kissing her with a damn tongue ring.

"Damn, Av's, are you sure?"

"Yeah, I want my tongue pierced."

"You got ID sweets? You gotta be eighteen for a piercing like that."

"Um, no I...I'm only seventeen," she blurts out innocently.

"Well, no can do, honey. Unless you got an adults permission."

"My brother here," she says elbowing me in the side, "is ok with it, so please sir?"

My stomach twists at her calling me her brother, but her eyes darting between the tattooist and me are eager and I'm willing to play along for her to get her tongue pierced.

"Yeah, man. I'm happy for my little sister here to get her tongue pierced."

"All sorted then. Give me ten to draw up your design and get the piercing gear ready."

The next hour or so passes by in a blur of pain. Ava sits beside me, clutching my hand when I wince slightly from the needles in my skin. It doesn't hurt much more than the acupuncture I had when I injured my back playing a rough game of basketball once.

Wicked Temptation

Her smile at the finished tattoo—over my shoulder blade, and onto my chest just above my nipple—makes me feel giddy.

It's open roses and a gardenia on a black background. My grandma, and mum's favourite flowers. And the intoxicating scent of her—my girl—my Ava.

"Zekey, I love it," she beams at me, kissing my cheek when I sit up to look at it in the mirror.

The tattooist—Billy—looks at us oddly, like he honestly doesn't believe our brother and sister story.

I don't blame him. He's got eyes and can obviously see the desire in our eyes for each other. I can't hide how I feel about Ava when we're not around family.

"Thanks Av's," I reply, smiling at her. "You ready for your tongue piercing?"

"Yeah, can you hold my hand?"

"Definitely," I reply, grabbing it, and sneakily pressing a kiss to the back of her palm whilst Billy's back is turned.

She lays down and opens her mouth, sticking her tongue out as he directs.

I try not to think about kissing her—knowing that will be off limits for awhile whilst it heals—and also to keep Z-man tame.

She squeezes my hand tight, wincing a little from the pain. And it's quickly over, with barely any bleeding.

He hands us both care instructions, I pay for both and lead Ava out of the shop with a hand on the small of her bare back. Z-man likes that. He's throbbing in my daks. And I wish I could kiss Ava, but can't right now.

Caz May

Getting home and walking into the house, we find Ashton pacing the open-plan space. His fists are clenched tight, as though he wants to punch someone. And he's obviously furious.

"Where the fuck have you been?" he bellows at us when we walk in, towards the kitchen. Ava is cowering behind me.

"We just went for a walk, bro," I say calmly, my hand behind my back brushing against Ava to keep her calm. "Chill yeah."

"Right chill," Ashton says rhetorically.

"Yes, Ashy, chill out man. You were busy. I just wanted to show Ava where we live."

"As if dickwad. You just wanted to get her alone for god knows what."

"No Ashton! I wanted her to not be alone because her brother is a fucking tool who didn't even say hello to her."

"I fucking did!"

I scoff at him. "In your fucking dreams Ashton. I don't even know who you are right now."

Ava moves from behind me, seething and breathing heavy. She's annoyed at Ashton and I don't blame her. She opens her mouth to say something, but no words come out from between her lips. She runs upstairs, to the bedroom, slamming the door behind her.

Again I scoff at my best mate who's completely dumbfounded like he doesn't know what's going on, nor what he's done to cause the reaction of his little sister.

"Well done, man. You upset Av's over nothing."

Wicked Temptation

He clenches his fists again, taunting me with them raised as though he's going to punch me. I couldn't give a flying fuck, although my tatt is a little tender so if he's going to hit me I hope he doesn't lay into my chest.

"You being around my little sister when you only think with your dick isn't nothing, Ezekiel." And there it is. Him calling me a manwhore again, making me wonder if he's suffered some freak accident and is now blind because he can't see how I feel about his little sister. It's either that or he doesn't want to admit that he knows how I feel and I'm good for Ava.

I don't have anything to say, nothing good at least, so I stay silent, and he continues to taunt me, "How does Devney feel about you and Ava spending time together?"

"She's cool Ashton, unlike you. Dev and I are friends," I tell him sincerely because it's true. Dev might want into my daks but in my eyes, nothing else sexual is going to happen between us.

"Yeah, whatever man. Keep ya shit up and we won't be friends."

Again I don't reply but scoff under my breath at his idiocy whilst I storm off to my room. At the landing, I think about going to see Ava but I don't.

Even though I desperately want to kiss her again I know I can't—because she just got her damn tongue pierced—and I'd have Ashton cutting my damn balls off.

Inviting Ava to stay—as well as Tempany—was a bad idea.

Thirty

Ava

Zeke's suggestion of going out for Mini golf should have been a good idea, but thanks to my idiot brother Zeke is on edge.

I can tell he wants to be close to me, wants to talk to me, but Ashton keeps giving us dagger eyes.

Tempany hip bumps him as we step up to the second hole.

Wicked Temptation

"Get a hole in one, Simba, and I'll give you a kiss."

My brother cracks a smile then. I don't get the whole Simba and temptress thing they have going on, but I don't question it. For some reason, it brings my brother back to earth and calms his rage.

"Damn, temptress, put the pressure on."

He stands at the tee, holding his golf club tightly and wiggles his butt as he hits the ball. Zeke calls out, "Miss, miss, fucker!"

Ashton hits the ball hard, and it completely misses the hole, jumping the barrier at the end. We all crack up laughing, Zeke doubling over and clutching his knees. Ashton gives him an up yours, waving his golf club towards his best friend.

"Calm ya tits, Ashy," Zeke taunts. "You could hurt someone waving ya club around like that."

Ashton stomps over to get his ball, and Zeke steps up behind me when I line up to hit next.

His front is pressed against my back, his dick pressing the curve of my bum. His arms wrap around my body, our fingers touching and holding the golf club together.

I was a terrible shot on the first hole, so bad I didn't even make contact with the ball. I instead hit the tee, snapping it in two.

It was partly deliberate, as I had a feeling Zeke wouldn't be able to stop himself from helping me hit a hole in one. But also other than basketball, I'm pretty hopeless at any other sport.

I'm loving having Zeke close, especially when he leans in to exhale a breath against my ear as he speaks, "Go for a slow and steady stroke, Ava."

Caz May

I love how he says my full name, helping me raise the golf club just slightly to hit the ball before he steps back. I hit it this time, and just enough that it rolls down the putting green and sinks in to the hole easily.

Ashton huffs, pulling Tempany against his side and kissing her temple. "It's on you now, temptress. Av's and Ezekiel are clearly cheating."

"You're just jealous that Av's and I are mini-golf pro's. You've always been hopeless at anything that requires you to use a stick correctly."

"Fuck you, Ezekiel!" Ashton roars.

"No thanks, Ashy, I'd rather fuck Ava," Zeke jeers, giving me a sexy wink that makes me tingle.

"You wouldn't dare, arsehole," my brother roars again, stomping towards Zeke like he actually is Simba come to life.

I've had enough. Zeke probably shouldn't bait him but still, Ashton has no right to be angry and making a scene in the middle of the mini-golf course.

"Ashton, stop, please. You're embarrassing us."

"Fine Av's, I'll stop, but tell me has he made any moves on you, for real?"

"No," I reply, shaking my head. "And what would it matter if he did?" I question, as Zeke walks away.

"You know he's not the guy for you, Av's."

I shake my head again, huffing and going to flirt with Zeke, who is sitting at a picnic table near the cafeteria.

"Sorry, he's such a dick."

"Don't apologise for your brother Av's."

"I know, but he shouldn't get so angry at you."

Wicked Temptation

"Right, but I love getting to him by getting all up close and personal with you, sexy."

I feel the blush rise up my cheeks, and can't help the giggle that escapes my lips.

"You think I'm sexy?"

"You Ava Castello, are sexy as fuck. Touch my dick and you'll see that just having you sitting so close to me makes me hard, baby."

I reach down, under the table and brush my hand across the front of his trackies. His dick is hard and throbs in my grip.

I murmur softly. He leans in to whisper in my ear, "Damn, Av's, I wish your mouth could be on Z-man whilst you make that noise."

I look into his denim eyes, that are focused on me, and reply seductively, "Maybe later, Ezekiel."

"Mmm, Ava...I. Can't. Wait," he teases, nibbling my ear a moment.

I stand up and head back over to my brother and stepsister.

I'm giddy just thinking about touching Zeke and sucking his dick. I've never sucked another guy off, and it's kinda exciting thinking about giving Zeke that first.

Hopefully, we can get a moment alone to explore each other without my brother being a raging bull pushing us apart.

Thirty-One

Ezekiel

Since Av's blatantly flirted with me at the mini golf course, mentioning that she literally wants to suck my dick I've been battling a hard on all arvo.

We're now all sitting in the lounge room watching a movie, Ashton & Tempany on the single seater couch--her on his lap--and Dev, Ava and myself are on the three seater.

Ava is next to me, her thigh pressing against mine, and we have a blanket over our laps.

Wicked Temptation

I don't know what shitty movie we're watching but I'm not watching it anyway.

Dev is the only one looking at the screen from time to time.

Ashton and Tempany are practically fucking each other, pashing like they're starving for each other.

I fucking get it. I'm starving for another taste of Ava's lips on mine.

She looks at me, before wrapping her ankle around mine and scooting even closer to me under the blanket. I lean into her side, exhaling a breath against her ear before whispering, "I want to touch your pussy, Av's."

She shivers, her eyes locking on mine and giving me the go-ahead with the way they're sparkling at me.

She nods towards Ashton, leaning close to whisper back, "What if Ashy sees?"

"He won't Av's. He's not watching the movie, let alone us," I tell her, clutching the edge of the blanket. I pull it up to our necks and slide my hand underneath it.

She squirms a little when my fingers brush against her stomach, before slipping inside her trackies, straight into her knickers. I flick the pad of my index finger over her clit and she shivers. She's wet and fuck it's hot.

I want to fucking taste her.

Slowly I slip a finger inside her pussy, still rubbing her clit whilst my eyes watch the pleasure overtaking her face.

She's trying not to move, but her hips buck up to take my finger in deeper. And leaning in I whisper, "Touch me, Av's."

Her eyes darken, her eyebrows raising at me as though a question is on the tip of her tongue, but she doesn't say anything before her hand is in my daks.

Her small hand starts rubbing over the front of my boxers, and Z-man is throbbing, hard as steel from just touching her, and having her hand against his fabric confines.

Again, hoping Dev can't hear me, I whisper to Ava, "Inside the boxers baby. I need your hands on me."

She bites her lip, sliding her hand into the waistband of my boxers.

And holy fucking shitballs. Fuck me fucking dead.

Her hand tentatively stroking Z-man makes me want to cream my daks like a teenage newbie touching his damn dick for the first time.

I slip another finger inside her pussy, pushing a finger up against her g-spot. And she comes—hard—squirming and biting down on her lip to hide the breathy *'fuck'* that threatens to escape as a scream.

I'm about to take out my finger and slip it in my mouth when Devney's eyes catch mine.

"Are you two alright?" she asks.

"Yep, yep, fine," Ava stammers. "I'm just going to get a drink. Anyone want anything?"

She stands up, the blanket nearly dropping to the floor before I quickly pool it at my lap to hide the tent in my daks.

Ashton and Tempany finally break their pash session and look towards us. Ashton answers Ava's question, "Nah, we're good."

I laugh. "The rest of us aren't. Could hardly hear the movie over you two sucking face."

"Up yours, Ezekiel," Ashton bites back, giving me the finger. Tempany licks his finger then, looking at him with a cheeky grin. I'm going to fucking chunder. They really need to go to his fucking room.

"Eww, man. You two make me wanna chunder. I'm going to go help Av's."

I expect him to bite back again, but instead, he's kissing Tem again, and she's practically fucking him by grinding her hips against his dick.

Standing up—thankful my dick has deflated for now—I head into the kitchen to find Ava leaning against the counter, sipping from a bottle of water.

She looks at me blushing as I step closer to her. Fumbling with screwing the lid back on she mutters, "Hey, Z."

"Hey, Av's. You ok?"

"Yep, better than ok."

"Really? You liked my hand in your knickers, making you come, huh?"

I cage her in, pressing her against the counter more. She bites down on her lip again, and with my forehead against hers I whisper against her lips, "I want to taste you, Ava."

She murmurs, just an 'mmm' escaping her lips. And I continue, "I want to fuck your mouth and your pussy with my tongue."

"We...we...shouldn't. Kiss. Zeke," she says raspy, not moving away from me.

Our breathing has increased, as well as my damn heart rate, not to mention that Z-man is growing harder by the second.

"Maybe not, Av's. But you know what?"

"What?" She whispers.

"Fuck it. Fuck it all, because I'm not waiting for a second longer to kiss you again."

And I don't—wait for a second—before crushing my mouth against hers.

She drops the water bottle on the floor, her hands moving up to brush against my neck and jaw as she licks my lips, begging for more.

I moan against her mouth, groaning as I grind into her body, Z-man creating friction between us.

This kiss is hot, everything, and turning me on more than ever.

Ava Castello is mine, made to kiss me into oblivion.

About to deepen the kiss with tongue—to fuck her mouth —I'm stopped, pulling back when I hear a voice behind us.

"Well, well, well. What's going on in here?"

I jump back from Ava, wiping my sleeve across my lips and looking at Dev as she saunters into the kitchen.

"Nothing Dev. Just grabbing a drink."

"Right, a drink," she says sarcastically, almost winking at me. "Because it looked like you were sneaking a kiss, and actually about to fuck against the kitchen counter."

"It wasn't what it looked like, Devney," Ava pleads, bending down to pick up her water bottle. "I dropped my water and Zeke tripped over it and fell against me."

Wicked Temptation

Devney laughs. "Yeah right. I'm not a fucking idiot. You were pashing."

"So what if we were Devney? It's none of your damn beeswax."

I like this side of Ava. Being all sassy bitch to Devney.

"Sure you weren't. Maybe I should just go and interrupt your brother from fucking his girlfriend on the couch and tell him that you were kissing just now?"

Ava shifts uncomfortably, stepping closer to Devney with lightning in her eyes. She's about to say something back but Devney doesn't let her. "Or maybe I should tell him about you feeling each other up on the couch instead? Bet he'd love that."

I ball my fists, seething and stepping in front of Ava who's about to launch herself at Dev. As much as seeing them bitch slap each other would be hot as hell, I can't let that happen. And I also can't let Devney tell Ashton anything.

"Please Dev, I'm begging you not to tell Ashton. He'll have my damn balls, and then my head."

She contemplates my words a moment, stepping closer to me.

"Well, maybe if you kiss me in front of Ava I won't tell."

"Oh come on, Devney. You're fucking shitting me."

"Nope," she says with a laugh, suddenly losing the distance between us before I even have a second to react. And kissing me. I hear Ava run off and shove Devney away.

"Fuck off, Devney! Seriously! You've fucked me the wrong way!"

She cackles like a fucking witch.

"I can fuck you anytime Zeke. And better than your virgin girl."

"Yeah, I think you should fuck yourself with a two inch dildo!" I bellow at her, storming out of the room to go after Ava.

Knocking on Ava's bedroom door she doesn't answer, but I can hear her sobbing. I'm irate, that Dev made my girl cry, but I know it's partly my fault too. I should've pushed Devney away quicker. But I didn't and now Av's is crying, and I need to grovel.

Opening the door, she's on the bed and looks up at me with tear stained cheeks. And fuck she's never looked more beautiful.

Kicking the door behind me, I practically sprint towards the bed and kneel on the floor.

Touching her hips I speak softly, "Av's please, look at me, baby."

"No," she snaps, the word muffled into the pillow she's sobbing into.

"Av's please, I'm sorry. So fucking sorry."

She's still sobbing, but her head turns to look at me. And my heart breaks when she mutters through her sobs, "After. We. Did. That...kissed. You. Kissed...her."

"I'm sorry Av's. Believe me. Kissing Dev is the last thing I want to do."

"But you did...kiss her."

"Av's come on. You know she kissed me. And no joke baby, you kissing me was a million times better. I want you, Av's."

Wicked Temptation

She sits up, clutching the pillow against her chest.

"You have a funny way of showing me that, Ezekiel."

God, it kills me when she calls me my full name. Hearing my full name fall from her full, kissable lips gets to me so much. It's like a hit of crack, if I was down with that shit.

"I'm sorry Ava, honestly. Please let me make it up to you," I beg, giving her a sexy smirk.

"How're you going to do that?" she taunts, trying to hide the smile that teases the corner of her lips.

"I have to show you," I tell her, standing up, and grabbing the pillow to throw on the floor.

"Oh," she mutters, blushing when I kneel on the edge of the bed.

Leaning down I kiss her, hard and passionately. Again her hands come up to grab my jaw and she moans against my lips as we fall together back on the bed. We keep kissing, and fuck it's ecstasy. No amount of kisses with Ava will ever be enough. I could kiss her all day, every day and it would still never be enough. But just kissing her isn't going to be enough to apologise for being a dick. And I honestly want to taste her properly.

Breaking the kiss, I smile at her.

"Fuck, Av's. I love kissing you, baby."

"Mmm, back at you Zekey. But you're not forgiven."

"Oh, well how about a kiss down under then?" I taunt, and her eyes light up.

"I've never done that."

"A first then," I tease with a wink, yanking her trackies and knickers down when I sit up.

Oh holy fuck, her bare pussy is fucking gorgeous.

She kicks the clothing off at her ankles and I throw it aside as I get on the bed, my head dipping straight between her legs that fall open for me. Without giving her any warning I lick her clit and she moans, calling out, "Fuck, Zeke!"

"You taste fucking delicious, Av's."

She giggles, and bucks her hips up when I slip two fingers inside her, teasing her g spot again as I kiss her clit again.

"Oh my god, Ezekiel! Feels so good."

Still touching her, I look up at her.

"Av's I want you to fuck my face with my tongue buried inside your pretty pussy."

"What? I..."

"Please, Av's. It will feel so good."

"Ok," she replies, blushing when I pull her up into my arms. I give her a cheeky kiss, and she licks her lips tasting herself on them.

"God, Av's. That's so sexy," I tell her sitting down on the bed and pulling down with me.

I lean against the headboard.

"Come here, baby. Put your pretty pussy on my face."

She follows the direction, and I lick her clit, before shoving my tongue inside her wet channel.

Holy shit, she tastes good.

Wiggling my tongue inside her she rocks her hips over my mouth and chin.

"Shit, Zekey," she calls out. "It feels so fucking good."

I pull back a moment, pushing a finger inside her.

"Come on my face, Av's, baby."

Wicked Temptation

I don't wait for a reply, kissing her clit again and lapping up her arousal like it's my last meal.

I've given plenty of Aussie kisses before but tasting Ava on my tongue, her fucking my mouth is by far the best one.

She rocks her hips—one last time—baring down on my mouth as I suck her clit and she explodes in a rush, coming all over my tongue and face with a bellowing, "Oh fuck, Zekey!"

Grabbing her hips, I move her down so she's sitting over Z-man who is rock hard. She doesn't say anything but kisses me softly.

"That was amazing, Zekey," she says with a smile, before kissing me again. "I guess you're forgiven."

"Glad you loved it. I'll be doing it again," I tease her giving her another kiss. "But I should probably head to bed before Ashton realises I'm not in my room."

"Yeah," she replies standing up and grabbing her discarded knickers off the floor and sliding them on.

Before heading out of her room, I kiss her again, wishing I could stay with her wrapped in my arms kissing her all night.

Closing Ava's bedroom door behind me I bump into Ashton who's come up the stairs as though he's on a mission.

"Did the movie finish?" I ask, trying to not act suspicious. He doesn't answer my question, instead asks another one, "Why are you coming out of Av's room?"

He's glaring at me, and I feel so guilty.

'Ah you know, just fucking your sister's pussy with my tongue.'

Yeah Nah, I don't say that.

"I heard her screaming or something. Was just checking she was alright."

I don't think Ashton believes me and I can still taste Ava on my lips, so I lick them and Ashton gives me dagger eyes, cocking his eyebrow at me.

"Right, man. Well, goodnight and maybe let Devney help her next time since she's in the next room."

I nod, half-arsed because I'm not letting Dev anywhere near my Ava.

"Yeah sure, man. Keep your sex noises on the down low tonight, yeah," I taunt him, nodding towards Tem when she comes up the stairs and steps up behind Ashton. She giggles at my words and leaving them be I go to my room to finish my night by jerking off whilst licking my lips to taste Ava's pussy on them still.

My head is pounding when I head into the kitchen the next morning. It's way to fucking early to be out of bed, but Dev is already up, sitting at the breakfast bar sipping a coffee. She eyes me as I grab a coffee too, heaping three spoonfuls of sugar into the mug, along with a dash of milk. I sip it and nearly spit it out at her when she blurts out, "I'm sorry about last night, Zeke."

"Um, yeah, thanks Dev."

"Did you apologise to Ava?"

"Yeah, all good. But that was a shit move Dev."

"I know. I'm really sorry."

"You know how I feel about her."

Wicked Temptation

"Yeah, honestly, I'm jealous. She's lucky."

She stands up when I don't reply and pulls me into a hug.

"We good?" she asks pulling back with a devious smile on her face that I don't like.

"Yeah, I guess. What're you smiling about?"

She nods towards the stairs. Ava is coming down and she looks cut.

Stepping into the kitchen, it's clear to see how upset she is with the tears stinging her eyes.

"You just can't help yourself," she says to Devney, wiping an arm across her cheeks.

"It's not what it looks like, Ava. I'm sorry for last night, and honestly, Zeke and I are just friends."

"I guess thanks," Ava says, stepping closer to me.

"I appreciate that. I shouldn't have kissed him in front of you."

"You shouldn't have kissed him at all."

"I know, and I'm sorry. I hope we can all be friends."

"I'd like that," Ava replies, and I pull her against my side, kissing her temple.

Devney smiles at us both as she walks out of the kitchen.

I give Ava a quick kiss. And she giggles at me.

"Good morning to you too, Ezekiel," she jeers at me, kissing me again.

"I could get used to kissing you, good morning, Av's. But Ash will be up soon, so you should keep ya pretty lips off me."

"It'll be a challenge but I'll try," she taunts, smirking at me. "What's for breakfast?"

"Coffee, and toast or cereal," I tell her, reaching up to the top cupboard to get out the Coco-pops.

She smiles at the breakfast cereal. "Ooo, coco-pops! My fave," she beams, grabbing a bowl and pouring some in, followed by some milk.

I give her a quick kiss on the forehead.

"I'm gonna go have a shower. Help yourself to anything, baby."

"Thanks, Zekey. Wish I could join you," she teases.

"Don't tempt me Av's," I reply laughing as I head out of the kitchen to the shower to once again wank to thoughts of her, this time thinking of fucking her under the spray of water. I've got it bad for my best mate's little sister. And I don't care what he thinks anymore, I'm going to make her mine completely.

Thirty-Two

Ezekiel

I can barely avert my gaze from Ava, as we all head down Queen Street towards the club in the city.

She's wearing a long sleeved sequinned little black dress with a scoop neckline. And it's so short it barely covers her pussy. It's fucking sexy how it exposes her long legs, and true to my girl she's paired it with high top black converse instead of the high heels I saw peeking out of her bag.

I'm surprised Ashton even let her walk out the door in the sexy outfit, let alone how cool, calm and collected he seems to be about taking his underage little sister to a nightclub.

Caz May

This one, Rhythm Lounge is know around campus to be a ripper hangout for getting tanked and dancing, and they're not strict on checking ID at the door; especially groups of guys and girls.

Still I'm nervous when we step up to the cue to get in. Ava shivers, standing in front of me, with Dev in front of her and Ashton & Tem behind me.

I step closer to her, wrapping my arms around her waist, my head resting on her head as we slowly start shuffling forward in line.

"Better, baby?" I ask with a whisper in her ear. She turns her head back to look at me, smiling and giving me a cute little nod.

And fuck I want to kiss her, but I can feel Ashton glaring at me from behind.

And he pokes me in the back, making me turn around to give him dagger eyes back.

"Hands to ya self wanker."

"Av's was cold, dufus. I promise my hands aren't in her sexy knickers."

"You wouldn't dare, Ezekiel." Little does he know. More than my hands have been near Ava's pussy, and I'm certainly thinking about finding out if she's wearing a g-string under her tight little black dress.

"Wanna tempt me, Ashton?" I jeer at him, raising my eyebrow at him cockily.

He's about to launch himself at me, but Tem pulls him back, whispering to him, "Down Simba."

He instantly calms, and kisses her, full on pda pashing.

Wicked Temptation

I honestly can't take much more of their loved up shit. It stirs my gut, because I'm so fucking jealous that I can't have that with Ava. I'm practically a green eyed rage monster, who wants to scream at my best mate admitting my feelings for his little sister.

But I can't, and having my arms wrapped around Ava's waist right now is probably the closest I'm going to get to her tonight.

Getting to the front of the line, we're ushered inside without a second glance and Dev rushes up to the bar, calling out, "I'll grab some shots and a jug of James Boer."

I give her a nod, taking Ava's hand and pulling her over to the booths I can see around the huge dance floor.

Music is blaring out, and it's classic old school songs that we'd sung not knowing the words as kids. Those songs that are so catchy but are full of dirty sexual innuendo.

Ash and Tem follow us, and we all slide into the booth. I'm happy Av's is sitting on the same side as me, and when Dev returns with the cowboy shots and the beers, I take a moment to glance down at Ava's thighs. Her dress has hitched up, and her pussy is practically on display. She's wearing a g-string for sure, and a dirty thought runs through my mind as I grab a shot with one hand, the other slipping between her legs to touch the soft inviting skin.

She grabs a shot and looks me dead in the eyes—whilst my hand is between her legs—as we both gulp down the cowboys shots, our eyes not leaving each others.

Putting the shot down on the table I lean into her and whisper, "Delicious, but you taste better."

She slaps my arm playfully. "Zekey, stop," she says with a giggle, nodding at Ashton across the table who is sipping a beer and giving me dagger eyes. And his eyes are stormier than usual.

If Tem wasn't sitting next to him I'd bet my balls he'd be beating me to oblivion for my flirting with Ava.

And I'm probably an idiot for what I'm about to say but I quite frankly want my best mate to fuck off for awhile. The music is thumping and I want to follow through on my earlier thought about touching Ava's sweet pussy. Dev is unusually quiet to, just sipping on a beer and not sure where to look.

"Ashy, you got a problem mate?"

"Yeah, I'm looking at him, Ezekiel."

"I'm not your problem. The fact is that even though all you've done these past few days is fuck Tem, and you're still wound to tight for your own fucking good."

"Yeah, go fuck yourself Ezekiel. Because you..."

I hate—absolutely detest—that he's berating me with my full name. He knows I hate being called 'Ezekiel' and still he taunts me with it.

But now him cutting his words off mid threat makes me want to hurl insults at him, tell him that I'll fuck Ava in front of him if he doesn't back the fuck down and stop acting like a lion set to kill me whenever I as so much look at his little sister.

I'm about to tell him that, even though it's a death wish when he stands up, pulling Tem up with him. She'd just whispered something in his ear and as usual, it calms him down. I couldn't give a flying fuck if it means I can be with Ava; alone.

Wicked Temptation

With a warning glare and an up yours from Ashton, he's dragged away to the dunnies by Tempany. And Devney stands up, laughing.

"I thought they'd never fuck off. They were killing my buzz."

"You're telling me, duchess."

"Oh you calling me that again huh? Ezekiel..."

"Don't you fucking dare, duchess. No one. No one calls me Ezekiel!" I bellow at her, squeezing Ava's thigh. Because only my girl—my Ava—can call me Ezekiel. It sounds deliciously sexy when she purrs my full name.

"Fine, but come on, let's dance," she singsongs waving her arms in the air and wiggling her hips seductively as she heads to the dance floor.

"Yeah, just give us a minute," I tell Dev, turning my attention back to my girl.

Brushing her hair out of her face, I kiss her, hard and teasingly by licking her lips.

Kissing Ava is better than any other high. Her kisses are fucking intoxicating.

Pulling back I look into her stormy eyes, cupping her cheek.

"Av's, you look so fucking sexy in this dress. Are you wearing underwear?"

"Maybe," she teases me with a smirk, opening her legs wider for my hand to slip between them more. And I come up against bare skin, her bare pussy.

"Av's, fuck baby. You're so damn dirty. I fucking love it."

Caz May

"I want you to touch me, Ezekiel," she purrs at me with a wink. And fuck, I practically come in my daks from that declaration. "And fuck me."

Oh fuck me dead.

"Av's," I murmur her name, kissing her before she can say anything else. "I want to fuck you so hard, but not here. Our first time won't be here in the booth of a nightclub."

She murmurs softly again, grabbing my neck to pull me back for another kiss that has me panting, completely lost in her.

I'm so fucking in love with her. And when I sleep with her it won't be fucking. Ava deserves so much more than that. If I wanted to fuck someone I'd have slept with Dev already.

Breaking the kiss Ava squeals, screaming out, "Oh my god, I love this song!"

Listening harder, I realise that 'Butterfly' by Crazy Town is playing and that earlier thought pops back into my head.

I stand up, holding out a hand to her, "Care to dance with me then, Av's?"

"Yes, yes," she shrieks, grabbing my hand and standing up, nearly showing the whole club a view of her pussy. Her pussy that is all mine.

Once on the dance floor I'm wedged between Devney and Ava. Ava's arms are wrapped around my neck and she's grinding her hips into me, rocking over my hard dick between us to the beat. I could lose myself, and fucking come like a horny teenager. Devney is grinding against my back but my focus is on Ava.

Wicked Temptation

Again I kiss her, sliding a hand down between our bodies to her pussy and slipping two fingers inside. She breaks the kiss, looking up at me with a mix of trepidation and lust in her eyes. She's so turned on, I'm sure my fingers pumping in and out of her pussy would be making a squelch sound if we could hear that over the music.

Her mouth falls open in an 'o' and leaning into her ear, I whisper yell—sing—the words of the song to her, *'Come come my lady, You're my butterfly, sugar baby, Come my lady you're my pretty baby, I'll make your legs shake, You make me go crazy.'*

She moans again, my fingers teasing her g-spot. Our bodies are still rocking together, and I can tell she's close. Her whole body is trembling. And her pussy is spasming, her climax building.

Smashing a kiss to her lips, I lick her lips and take her tongue with mine, loving the sensation of her tongue ring against my lips and tongue as I fuck her mouth. And as the final bars of the song ring out, her legs shake and she comes with a moan against my mouth. Breaking the kiss, I pull my fingers out, and put them up to her lips to taste. She licks them, and I groan from frustration but also because her licking the taste of her pussy off my fingers is the hottest fucking sight ever.

"Fuck, Av's. Fuck."

I kiss her again, so hard and dirty our mouths are practically one. But the kiss is cut short when I feel Dev tugging on my jacket and pulling me away.

I look back at her, anger flaring.

"What the fuck Dev?"

"Brother incoming," she yells at me, nodding towards the other side of the dance floor.

Ava's eyes lock on Ashton and Tempany, and she doesn't even look at me as she runs back over to the booth and grabs a beer, gulping it down like it's water.

I turn back to Dev, and start dancing with her. I've made a big mistake—even though it feels like the complete opposite—and I need to get drunk and stop thinking about how insanely fucking good being with Ava feels.

Wicked Temptation

Thirty-Three

Ava

After walking away from Zeke on the dance floor, my legs are jelly, and my core is still pulsing from the dirty orgasm he gave me.

I'd hoped my brother didn't see the kiss we shared after, as he's heading right towards me, and even though he's probably

Caz May

had the anger fucked out of him, he still looks like he wants to murder his best friend. And that's on me.

I can't be with Zeke, because ultimately we're both going to be crushed. Zeke's ego, and my heart.

Pouring a glass of beer, I gulp it down. It tastes like vomit, but I need to get drunk, and fast. I follow it with another, trying to not think about the fact that Zeke is now dancing with Devney and he's discarded me, like he didn't just kiss me and bring me almost to my knees on the dance floor moments ago.

He's the only one who can make me feel. But clearly it's one sided. And I'm ruined for anyone else.

Ashton comes over to the table.

"Ava you need to stop drinking."

"No, I'm getting drunk brother. Isn't that what you're supposed to do at club?"

"Not when you're seventeen, Ava."

I don't reply, instead I walk up to Zeke and pull him away from Devney. He turns to me, his eyes lighting up.

"What's wrong Av's?"

"I need you to get me drunk."

"Why?"

"Because my brother is an arse."

"You got that right. What you want to drink?"

"Anything," I tell him, linking my arm with his as we head over to the bar.

I want to piss my brother off. And getting drunk and making a scene with his best friend is bad, but the best way.

Wicked Temptation

Zeke orders a couple of shots of peppermint vodka and we down them together. The burn followed by the sweet minty taste is divine. And I signal for another one, downing that and starting to feel the buzz of the alcohol in my veins.

It makes me feel giggly.

"You're drunk Av's," Zeke tells me with a chuckle, taking my hand and leading me back towards my brother, Tempany and Devney.

"We should get out of here and get some food. I'm starved," Zeke announces, rubbing his stomach. He quickly downs the last of the beer on the table.

"Sounds ripper, but you need to keep ya hands to yourself," Ashton says, taking Tempany's hand to follow Zeke and I out. "Dev, you coming?"

"Nah, I'm going to meet up with some other friends. I'll see you at home."

"No worries," Zeke tells her, and we head out of the club.

"So TGI Fridays at Central?" Ashton asks, heading across the road to the tram stop.

"Oh yes, they place is grouse."

We all get on the tram that pulls up and Zeke pulls me close against him as we stand by the doors in the full tram.

I'm still all giggly, and he laughs at me. "You drunk Av's?"

"Yeah, you?"

"Yeah, buzzed baby. And if hover brother wasn't next to us I'd be pashing you right now."

Hover brother. I snort with laughter at that comment.

But I don't get to reply as the tram is stopping and Ashton and Tempany are jumping off. We head into the large shopping mall, towards a set of escalators that aren't working.

"Oh shit," Ashton says, looking around for another way to get to the restaurant up the top of the building.

"There's an elevator around the corner," Zeke says and we all head around there.

Getting in, Zeke is being weird, undoing his jeans for some reason. Ashton and Tempany start laughing with me, at Zeke oddly trying to lighten the moment. And it's then I realise his dick—his hard glorious dick—is out of his jeans, in his hand and he's spinning it around calling out, "Woo!" at the top of his lungs.

He steps up to the buttons, and hollers, "Going up!" before pushing the elevator button with his dick…

"No Zekey what are you doing?" I call out.

Tempany calls out from behind me, "Oh my god, Zeke, what the fuck are you doing!? Stop!"

Zeke is cacking himself laughing, pressing the tip of his dick against all the buttons and spinning it around like an idiot.

It's absolutely hilarious, and fucking sexy.

Even my stuck up brother is laughing. And as the elevator starts moving Zeke turns to look at us, taking a bow before putting his dick back in his pants.

"Thank you, thank you. I'm here all week," he says with laugh that makes us all erupt into laughter, absolutely shitting ourselves.

Wicked Temptation

I'm not hungry for food now, but I want to taste Zeke's dick; after he's had a shower of course. So maybe some food might not be so bad; for now.

Thirty-Four

Ezekiel

After we get home, I head straight to the shower to wash my dick from the elevator scum. The way Ava had looked at my dick when I did that was a mix of horror and desire. And I'd sported a semi for the rest of the night.

Stroking myself in the shower—thinking of her touching me—didn't even calm me and now in bed I'm tossing and turning, fighting my pillow to make me close my eyes, but it's useless. Sleep isn't going to come tonight.

Wicked Temptation

Getting out of bed, I tug on some trackies and pull a t-shirt from the floor over my head. I don't bother with shoes or even socks and heading out to the kitchen for a drink I curse myself for that as the floorboards are as cold as ice on the balls of my feet.

Searching through the cupboards for a few minutes, I finally find the tin of milo and grab a mug and teaspoon, scooping in three heaped spoonfuls. I flick the kettle on to boil, leaning against the counter to wait for it to pop.

Rubbing my eyes, I'm sure I'm seeing things, because there's no way Ava is coming into the kitchen wearing only a t-shirt.

She steps up to me, and my heart kicks into high gear. She's so beyond beautiful. And she's giving me a sweet—sexy—smile.

God I fucking love her.

"Hey," she says softly, blushing.

"Hey, Av's. Couldn't sleep either, huh?"

"No, I kept thinking about kissing you. And I went into your room but you weren't there."

"Thinking about kissing me huh?" I tease, looking her sexy body up and down. Z-man suddenly tents my daks.

"Yeah," she mutters softly, stepping closer to me so she's within my reach.

Grabbing her by the hips I pull her close, whispering against her lips, "I've been thinking about kissing you to, Ava. Kissing every inch of you, until you scream my name."

Caz May

She whimpers, a sexy murmur and then we're kissing again, devouring each other as though this will be our last kiss.

Still kissing her I pick her up and put her down on the edge of the island bench. Her legs open for me and stepping in between them, my hard dick brushes against her naked pussy.

Pulling back from the kiss I'm breathless.

"Damn, Firefly. I want you."

She gives me an odd look at the nickname I just called her. I can't explain why that just escaped my lips but I'm definitely calling her it again.

Her eyes are staring into mine, and my heart is pounding, skipping a beat when she says raspy, "Fuck me Zekey bear."

Oh fuck me, I love when she calls me Zekey. And adding bear to the end of that nickname just makes it so much sweeter.

I kiss her again, whispering against her lips, "Not here Av's."

She wraps her legs around my arse and lifting her off the bench I carry her upstairs, kissing her until we get to my room.

Closing the door behind me with a kick, I break the kiss as I put her down on my bed. She splays her arms out, making the t-shirt ride up to show her bare pussy. I never knew my Av's was so damn naughty, and fuck me, it turns me on. Z-man is rock hard, practically pushing my daks down to get out of the confines.

We start kissing again and strip each other, until we're both completely naked. Ava looks at Z-man, licking her lips

Wicked Temptation

when she grabs him and starts to stroke my hardness. Her hands feel amazing on me. So fucking amazing I could come just from her touch.

"Zekey, please," she begs, opening her legs wide for me to touch her pussy. She's so wet.

"Zekey, I want you to fuck me," she declares with a sexy smirk.

"Are you sure Ava? I don't want to hurt you," I tell her, leaning down to give her a soft kiss.

"You won't. I'm not a virgin Ezekiel," she tells me, seeming really forlorn.

"What's bad about that?" I ask worriedly.

"I should've waited for you."

"Don't say that Av's. I can fuck you harder. And damn do I want to."

She pulls me down for a hard kiss, that makes Z-man throb. I'm desperate for her kiss, desperate to be inside her to make her mine.

Breaking the kiss, I murmur against her lips.

"I need you Ava. Please?"

She giggles sweetly and it makes Z-man throb again.

"Condom?" she asks. I don't respond. If I do it would be to blurt out that I want to fuck her bare, but the fact she's asking about protection most likely means she's not on the pill. And wearing a condom is probably best, as I honestly don't think I'll be able to pull out.

Getting off the bed I grab one out from my wallet on the floor, that's in the pocket of my jeans.

I throw it at Ava on the bed, and she giggles as she rips the foil open, beckoning me back to the bed with a curled finger and sexy smirk. She slides it on, stroking my dick at the same time.And I kneel in between her legs pushing them apart and bending her knees back so I have a clear view of her bare pussy.

"Are you sure Av's?"

"Yes, Ezekiel, I'm sure. Fuck me please, Ezekiel." Hearing her beg for my dick to be inside her, using my full name makes my whole body hum.

Without warning, knowing her pussy is deliciously wet I plunge my dick into her.

Starting to thrust in and out, her hips rise to take my dick in deeper, and she's moaning her pleasure loudly. I'm loving how I'm completely filling her and can see my dick disappear inside her all the way, so there is no space between us.

"Av's I want you to ride my dick."

Her eyes light up and I give her a kiss, still pumping my dick inside her as I roll us over so she's on top of me. I probe inside her and she starts to rise her hips up to ride me, taking my dick deeper inside her.

It's fucking ecstasy. Fucking amazing.

The best sex of my entire fucking life. She's moaning, panting, calling out, "Zeke, fuck. Fuck. So good."

I brush a finger over her clit and she bares down on my dick to meet my thrusts.

Sitting up with her still riding me so she's sitting in my lap —and I'm filling her—I kiss her and whisper against her lips, "Come for me Ava. Come on my dick."

Wicked Temptation

She takes me all the way out and then slams back down, taking me deep inside, making her pussy spasm with a quivering orgasm that has her trembling in my arms as I pump my release inside her.

She collapses against my chest, as I fall back on the bed, pulling her with me. And she slides off, laying down next to me. I yank the condom off, throwing it on the floor and wrap an arm around her body next to me.

"Fuck Ava," I verbalise, kissing her cheek. "Why'd we wait so long to fuck?"

"I don't know," she replies, shaking her head a little at me. "I'm sorry I didn't save my first time for you," she tells me again, her eyes on me full of sincerity.

I don't care that she wasn't a virgin for me. Quite frankly I'm glad, because I got to fuck her harder.

"Honestly firefly, it's ok," I tell her, kissing her with vigour before adding, "But I'm the only one who's going to fuck you now."

She lets out her sweet giggle again, asking, "Why're you calling me firefly?"

I shift a little on the bed so I'm facing her and looking into her stormy eyes when I say, "You light up my world Ava Darby Castello." I kiss her. "That's why."

She smiles at me, so wide my heart swells with love for her.

"Yeah well, you're my Zekey bear because I'll never forget our first kiss. Or tonight either. I lo…" I silence her with another kiss, murmuring against her lips, "Don't firefly. Don't tell me those words."

"But I feel them," she says abruptly, with her cheeky defiance.

"I know but if you tell me that and Ashton finds out I fucked you...I..." I can't finish the sentence. It hurts to much.

I can't be with her after tonight and my heart is breaking, more so when she softly mutters, "I know."

I pull her close again, so she's lying in my arms. My heart is beating really fast and the stabbing pain hits me like a knife to the chest. It's so unbearable—more than it ever has been—making me shift next to her.

"You ok, Zekey bear?" She questions me, giving me a worried gaze. Brushing her off I tell her, "I'm fine Av's. You just ignite my heart."

"Aww, Zekey bear," she says in a hushed tone, giving me a kiss again that shatters me completely. *I love you, Ava.*

"You're my firefly, Ava, lighting up my world."

She blushes, kissing me again before we close our eyes to fall asleep in each other's arms.

Wicked Temptation

Thirty-Five

Ava

Waking up in Zeke's arms the next day is surreal. The way he'd made me feel, his words that set my heart alight but broke it at the same time, and the sex between us.

After my first time with Drake, I didn't honestly think sex could feel so amazing. But with Zeke it was incredible. I still regret not saving my first time for him, but at the same time I don't think it would have felt anywhere as good and for that I'm glad.

Zeke has his arm over me and he softly murmurs in his sleep, as I lift it off and climb out of his bed.

I'm tempted to kiss his forehead, but I'm worried he'll wake up. Instead I pull on my discarded t-shirt from on the floor.

Tiptoeing out of the room, I open the door slowly and bump into Tem as she's heading out of Ashton's room.

She gives me a cheeky smile as we head downstairs.

"Morning Av's," she says to me, noticing how giddy I am. "Something happen last night?" she adds, getting out some cereal when I sit on the breakfast bar stool.

"I...um...I..."

"What? Did you sleep with Zeke?"

"Yeah, we um..."

"You fucked him?"

"Yeah, Tem and it was amazing."

"I bet it was. Maybe you should tell Ashton how you feel."

She puts a bowl in front of me with a spoon and the bottle of milk from the fridge.

Starting to spoon the Coco Pops into my mouth I shake my head, blurting out between mouthfuls, "I can't do that."

"Why?" Tem asks, eating a spoonful of her own bowl of Coco Pops.

"Because it doesn't matter. Zeke is pushing me away again anyway."

"Oh? How?"

"Yeah, he just keeps saying we can't be together. Even after last night."

"You need to talk to him Av's. Don't let him push you away."

I push my half eaten bowl of Coco Pops away, feeling a rush of nausea hit me. Just the thought of telling Zeke how I really feel, and having him push me away again turns my stomach.

"Yeah I guess," I mutter, swallowing hard to try and quell the nausea. "Can you distract Ashton later?"

"You bet," Tem replies with a smile and we laugh together.

"I'm so glad you're my sister Tem," I tell her standing up and hugging her. "And I honestly hope I find love like you and Ashton have."

"You will," she tells me with her sweet smile again.

She's honestly like the older sister I never had and always wanted. I love my brother, but he can be a real douche canoe sometimes, especially when it comes to my love life. And I know he's trying to be protective, but it's not his place.

Dad might have been a dick of a father, but sometimes Ashton is a dick of a brother when it comes to my feelings. I'm sure he'd probably have a heart attack if I told him I'm in love with Zeke, let alone that I fucked him.

I focus back on Tem, who is now sipping on her coffee. And holding a cup out to me.

"You want a coffee?"

"No, I'm ok. Do you really think I'll find someone who loves me like my brother loves you?"

"Yeah I do and I'm pretty sure you have that with Zeke. He's just not good at expressing it."

"Yeah, maybe. I hope so. Because I love him so much."

"I know, Ava. I can tell by the way you look at him when you think no one is looking."

I feel the blush rise up my cheeks.

"It's a pity he doesn't feel the same way."

Tempany laughs sweetly.

"I wouldn't be so sure about that. He looks at you in the same way. Like you light up his world."

I spit out the spoonful of milk from my mouth. And Tempany is glaring at me.

"What'd I say?"

"He said that to me last night."

"Well, there you go. What'd I tell you. Speak to him Ava."

"I will," I reply, finishing off my Coco Pops when speak of the gorgeous devil he saunters into the kitchen wearing only grey trackies.

I don't know where to look—at the glorious outline of his dick—or at his gorgeous face with the cheeky smirk.

My stomach flip flops, and I swallow hard to not just race up to him and jump into his arms as I kiss him.

I'm so hopelessly in love with Ezekiel Alessio.

He's my wicked temptation, that I want more than anything to give into again, but until I tell him how I feel I can't let anything else happen between us.

Wicked Temptation

Thirty-Six

Ezekiel

Waking up in pain again I clutch my chest, thumping a fist against my heart to try and stop it from getting worse, maybe make the blood pump better.

My heart hurts from more than this pain that's been annoying the shit out of me though. It hurts because I love Ava so much. And that's the sole reason I'm pushing her away a bit.

I'm fucking scared shitless that my heart is fucked; like surgery fucked again. I can't let Ava in—to let her love me— when I'm probably going to leave her heartbroken.

Caz May

I'm surprised that she's not still in bed with me, and that her shirt is gone from the floor as well.

Last night was in-fucking-credible. Absolutely, the best fucking sex of my life and damn I would've loved to sink inside her—preferably bare—this morning, but no such luck for Z-man who is already painfully hard just thinking about last night.

Ava riding the Z-train has ruined Z-man for life. No other pussy will ever feel the same.

Sighing at my misfortune I get up, yanking on some grey trackies before I head downstairs to find Ava in the kitchen talking to Tem whilst they're eating breakfast. She looks absolutely stunning, fresh faced and fucking beautiful. My heart hammers in my chest again. And I want to stalk across the room to kiss her, not giving a fuck that Tempany would get a show and see me acting all caveman *'I want Ava, now'.*

When I get closer I jeer at them, "Talking about me?"

I throw in a smirk for good measure, making sure my tone is jovial.

"No, why would we be talking about you?" Ava asks, laughing.

"Because you think I'm sexy," I taunt back, winking at her and then at Tempany who can't stop laughing.

"You sexy?" Ava teases, standing up from the breakfast bar stool so she's in my personal space.

"You're not sexy, Ezekiel. Not one little bit," she tells me cupping Z-man in her hand and squeezing him. She leans up to whisper in my ear then, "But I loved riding your dick last night."

Wicked Temptation

I choke on my own damn spit.

"Um shit, Av's. Kill me why don't you?"

"Yeah, nah, then I couldn't fuck you again," she taunts me, stretching up on her tiptoes to press a kiss against my lips.

I don't let her break it, but kiss her harder, only pulling back when Tem clears her throat to interrupt us.

"You might want to lay off on the pda just in case Ashton gets his lazy butt out of bed."

I step back from Ava, laughing. "Did you fuck him to hard last night?"

"Might have. But it's not your beeswax, Ezekiel," Tem taunts me with a cheeky smile.

"I honestly don't wanna know. As long as you keep ya pretty mouth shut about me and Av's, we're good."

"Not my place to tell Ash that. But you should own up to him."

"Yeah, not going to happen. He thinks I'm still heartbroken about Lorena."

Av's is glaring at me like she's going to cry. Putting an arm around her waist, I squeeze her against my side, kissing her temple.

"Oh," Tem replies gulping.

"Speaking of Lorena, how's she doing?"

Tem eyes me. "Good I guess, considering you broke her heart, dufus."

"Yeah, I...never meant to hurt her. She's a good one. Say hi for me."

"Yeah, sure. Anyway, I'll leave you two to chat."

She walks out of the kitchen, and I'm tempted to shove Ava against the kitchen bench for a sneaky fuck, but she's looking at me like I've broken her heart.

She's really upset, and I'm worried she's regretting last night.

"Av's you ok?"

"Yeah, well, nah."

"Do you regret last night?"

"No, but..."

"But what Av's?"

"You said we can't be together."

"Well, yeah, nah we can't. You know that."

"I want to be with you Zekey bear. Who cares what my brother thinks?"

"I do firefly. He'll kill me. And honestly that's not the reason we can't be together. I'll hurt you."

She's still standing too far away from me, looking so shattered I just want to pull her into my arms to kiss her until we can't breathe and tell her that I love her.

I know I'm probably overthinking about my heart, the worst case scenarios happening. But I don't want to bother anyone about it either. I'm fine otherwise and it's probably nothing but stress from uni. It will pass like it always has.

"You don't get to decide that, Ezekiel."

"Av's please," I beg, grabbing her and pulling her close to me. "We can't be together. Don't make this any harder than it needs to be."

"Don't you care about me, at all?"

Wicked Temptation

"Of course I fucking care about you, firefly," I tell her, looking into her dark stormy eyes that are locked on me with tears in the corners. Brushing them away with my thumb I continue, "And that's why we can't be together."

I'm trying to tell her *'I love her'* without actually saying the words. It's not working, and she pulls away from me, rushing up the stairs without even looking at me.

My heart pounds in my chest, another pain surge hitting me. Might as well let it take it me away, because without Ava in it, my life isn't worth living.

She's my firefly, and my damaged heart will always belong to her.

Thirty-Seven

Ava

Lugging my bag out to Tem's car, I don't even want to look at Zeke.

I love him so much, but I hate him for pushing me away when we shared something so special I can still feel my body aching from his touch days later.

Wicked Temptation

Shoving my bag into Tem's car I give my brother a quick hug, leaving him to say goodbye to Tempany with a kiss that should be behind closed doors.

I want to kiss Zeke goodbye, but I can't. I lean against the car to wait for Tempany, trying to hold back my tears, but it's no use.

Zeke comes sauntering out of the house, his eyes locked on me, and the tears start cascading down my cheeks. He steps up to me, completely ignoring the fact that my brother is a mere metre away from us—otherwise occupied—but not completely oblivious.

Zeke pulls my body to his in a hug.

"Av's," he murmurs softly in my ear before kissing my forehead.

I want to shove him away, tell him to go fuck himself, but fuck being in his arms feels so good; so right. He pulls back a little from me, so our eyes catch each other. And brushing the tears from my cheeks with his thumb he softly says, "Be good, firefly."

And before I can reply, or even think he walks away, not even giving me another look.

My heart shatters. I want to sink to the ground and have it open up and swallow me whole. I'm distraught.

He's acting as though nothing happened between us, that we didn't have sex that was far more than a release.

Thankfully Tem has opened the car, so yanking the door open I slide into the passenger seat and let the tears fall, glad her little Fiat has tinted windows so my brother can't see me falling apart because I'm hopelessly in love with his best friend; who just broke my heart completely.

Ten minutes later, Tem finally gets in the car to drive home to Lockgrove Bay. She doesn't say anything to me, just concentrates on driving in the city traffic until we're out on the main highway.

I've still got tears in my eyes. And I hate that I'm crying for Zeke. He doesn't deserve my tears, nor my heart that he has such a hold on it feels like it's being squeezed inside my chest with every wretched sob that escapes my mouth.

I'm shocked, hiccuping when Tem suddenly says, "Av's you have to move on."

"I..." Hiccup.

"If you told him how you feel and he's still pushing you away, as much as I care for Zeke he's not worth your tears."

I nod, holding my breath and counting to thirty to stop my hiccups.

"I know. But I didn't really tell him that I love him," I tell her, taking another deep breath. I wonder if the hiccups mean he's thinking about me, but I shake the ridiculous thought away. "And the thought of letting go of him makes my heart hurt like he's ripped it out."

"I know Av's," Tem replies, smiling at me. "Just think about it. I don't like seeing you so upset."

"Thanks, Tem. I love you, big sis."

I give her a big smile, wiping my arm across my cheeks. I mean my words to her. I'm so beyond glad to now have a sister, and I hope that maybe she can talk some sense into my brother.

"Aww, Ava. I love you too. We're family, always."

"Yeah, do you think you could talk to Ashy for me?"

"About Zeke?"

"Yeah. He'll listen to you."

"Yeah, I guess I can try. But you should too."

"I know," I reply nodding, before reaching down to turn on the radio. "But now I think we need some tunes."

"Couldn't agree more," Tem replies, laughing and nodding.

And my heart pounds and shatters when the song blaring out of the radio is, 'I believe in a thing called love' by the Darkness.

I love this song, and singing out the words I wonder if Zeke believes in love as much as I do.

Thirty-Eight

Ezekiel

All I've done since the girls left four days ago is wallow in my own self-pity in bed, still smelling Ava on my sheets; which I should have changed.

But I'm missing Ava like she's honestly yanked my fucked up heart out of my chest and taken it home to Lockgrove Bay with her. Back home with her where it belongs. She fucking owns my heart and I'm the fucking idiot who pushed her away without telling her how much I fucking love her.

Wicked Temptation

I grab my phone, my finger hovering over the FaceTime button to call her, but I can't. I need to give her space. To forget about what happened between us.

Instead of calling her, I text Dane. I've missed my big brother so much since he'd pissed off to the army.

Bro...can you chat? All good if you can't.

YEAH, LITTLE BRO. HIT ME UP.

I dial his number, and he answers straight away in his usual chipper tone, "Hey little dufus. How's the big smoke?"

"Shit bro. Now Av's is gone."

"Oh...yeah, what happened?" he enquires, as though he's smiling. "You've been holding out on me, huh?"

"Yeah, she came to visit for the holidays." I gulp, not sure if I can confess my feelings to my older brother now I've got him on the line after months without speaking to him.

"And what? Did she tell you she's in love with you?"

I gasp, flabbergasted.

"What? Av's doesn't love me."

"Are you blind little bro?"

"No. But..." I pause, contemplating his words.

"What happened with you guys?"

Ok, big boy daks. Tell him, Ezekiel. Big bro advice is what you need.

"We slept together, but I pushed her away. I can't be with her bro. Ashton will have my balls if he finds out."

"Yeah but Ezekiel, do you love her bro?"

"Yeah, so fucking much. It's always been Ava. And being with her feels so right, but it's wrong."

I can hear my big brother practically shaking his head at me for being daft.

"Well, bro, I hate to cut this convo short, but my drill Sergeant is ragging me. Man up. And tell her."

"Yeah…bye D."

"Bye bro," he replies as he hangs up.

I throw my phone on the floor, beating my fists against the bed. It doesn't make me feel any better. And it only tortures me more, as the scent of Ava—gar-fucking-denia—wafts up to my nostrils and I want to choke and suck in the scent into my lungs and die from inhaling it at the same time. I have to get out of this room, right fucking now.

Getting up, I pull on a t-shirt and run downstairs to the kitchen. I grab a beer, gulping it down in a haste, barely tasting it.

I just want to get drunk, and forget. Pass out. Die. And forget the pain of Ava yanking my fucking heart out, and the pain of my heart just being a complete fucking wanker and useless shitty organ.

Throwing the empty beer bottle in the rubbish, I get down a glass from the top shelf and pour myself a glass of whiskey.

I down that and then another in quick succession, about to down another when Dev comes home, sauntering into the kitchen with a devilish smirk.

She eyes the half empty whiskey bottle I'm clutching in my clenched fist.

Wicked Temptation

"Hey," she purrs at me, leaning in to grab the whiskey from me. "Leave some for me."

"Hey, Dev," I reply in greeting as she puts the bottle to her lips, taking a big swig.

"What are we drinking to?" she asks, licking her lips and handing the bottle back to me.

I take another big swig, until there is hardly anything left and reply, "To forget Dev."

"Right. Well, I'm down for that," she tells me as she grabs a beer out of the fridge. And drinks it eyeing me. She lets out a sudden laugh, looking at me like I've grown a second head.

"Are you crying right now, Zeke?"

"Nope. Just got something in my eyes," I lie through clenched teeth, turning away from Dev's prying eyes.

"What you thinking about?"

"What do you think, Dev," I snap, taking a final swig of the whiskey and slamming it down on the bench, wondering what it would sound like if it shattered into a thousand pieces like my shattered heart.

"Her."

"Nailed it. And yeah..." Fuck I need more whiskey.

"I can help you forget her. Get you off."

I shake my head, feeling chunder rising from the pit of my stomach. "Yeah, no thanks."

"Suit yourself." And she goes upstairs, whilst I grab out another beer to keep drinking.

Half an hour later I'm so fucking drunk, I can't see straight. I'm stumbling up the stairs, taking them two at a time, straight to her door.

Forgetting is what I need to do.

To feel some pleasure and not this overwhelming pain. I don't say anything, just stalk in like a predator and I find her lying on my bed scanning her phone in her hand.

She gives me some weird look, but her eyes rake my body. And I don't let her think before I'm on her bed and I kiss her.

It feels good, a release. I can't lie and say she can't kiss. Cause Dev can kiss and I'm getting carried away.

Z-man is throbbing—probably from thinking about someone else—but still, he's hard and I'm drowning in a kiss.

I'm not sure how it happens—when it happened—mid kiss but Dev is now naked and I'm only in my boxers.

"Zeke, please," she begs me as I start kissing her tits, and over her bare stomach.

"Pl..ea..se...wh...wh...at?" I slur, letting out a burp. She laughs at me, shoving my head towards her pussy.

"Kiss me, Zeke," she demands.

"Wh...wh...ere?" I slur again, shoving a finger into her pussy. *Damn, she's a loosey goosey.*

Not like my Av's tight pussy at all. Z-man throbs with the memory of Av's tight pussy.

"Don't tease me, Zeke."

"Ok..ies," I tell her, kissing her clit.

She moans and I lick her channel. Tastes good, but nothing like my Av's sweet as fuck pussy.

Wicked Temptation

Devney writhes on the bed beneath my tongue and it seems like only a second before I feel her pussy pulse with her release.

Pulling back I choke on the assault of her climax on my tongue, spitting a plethora of saliva over her stomach.

Why the fuck did I just do that?

God, I licked Dev's cunt. Fuck!

Regret hits me in the chest and without picking up my t-shirt I stumble out of her room to mine.

Falling against my bed I pass out. And hope I choke on the regret so I never have to face Ava again and tell her that I'm a monumental fuck up who put my mouth—that should only touch her—on some other chicks pussy.

You're a fucking idiot Ezekiel Stefan Alessio.

A hopeless fucking wanker in love with a girl I'll never be able to have.

Thirty-Nine

Ezekiel

Next day waking up I stretch, rolling over in bed to find Dev is in bed with me. I'm still only in my tight white boxers, and Dev is fucking starkers.

My head is fuzzy, and pounding from the hangover I've inflicted on myself.

Z-man is hard, so I don't think I've fucked Devney. If I'd have gotten off during the night he'd be tame. I don't recall much from the night before, except going down on Dev and passing out, and then I'm sure I dreamt of Ava.

But now, in my groggy hungover state I have no idea because Devney is touching Z-man through my boxers, stroking him to attention more.

I glare at her.

"Um, Dev. What the fuck are you doing?"

"You want to repeat last night?" she asks, giving me a wink.

"Nothing happened last night, did it?"

"You tell me, Zeke, but from what I remember it felt so good."

Fuck. Did I fuck her? I can't remember anything from after I left her room.

"Did we fuck? Cause if we did Dev, it's not happening again."

"Of course we did. It felt so good, Ezekiel."

She's fucking teasing me. She has to be fucking baiting me.

"You're shitting me Dev, right?"

She tries to kiss me, but I manage to put my hand over my mouth. "Don't, Dev. Tell me you're fucking shitting me?"

"Fine, we didn't fuck. But you give great Aussie kisses."

I try to recall the night before in my head, swallowing hard to shove the regret down. My mouth shouldn't have been anywhere near Dev's lips, or her pussy.

"Fuck! I...fuck!" I curse out, shoving my hands into her as I get up, not caring that she falls to the floor in a tangle of my bed sheets.

"Come on Zeke. She's gone. I'm here and you need to stop acting like a lovesick tosser."

My head is spinning, her words 'she's gone' tumbling in my mind. Ava might be gone but that doesn't mean I'm moving on. And that wouldn't be happening with Devney, even if she paid me.

"Get out! I don't want you here!" I bellow at her, stalking around the bed, and yanking the sheets away from her.

She's started to sob, but I don't give a flying fuck. She scrambles to get up, her mouth opening and then closing as though she can't form a sentence.

I don't care. Care factor zilch.

"Seriously Devney, get the fuck out of my fucking house!"

Somehow she finds her feet, and runs out of my room in tears.

I feel so shit. Like I've cheated on Ava when I know I haven't.

Grabbing the sheet from the floor, I toss it across the room, ripping the fitted one off the bed and throwing that as well. My bed doesn't smell like Ava anymore. And I fucking miss her.

Lying back on the mattress of the stripped bed, I grab my phone from the bedside table and text Ava.

Miss you firefly

She doesn't reply—but it says read—so I type another one.

Wish I could lick and fuck your pussy right now

I put my phone down, closing my eyes and sliding a hand into my boxers to wank.

Forty

Ava

Running down the stairs my phone vibrates for a second time in my hand. The text messages from Zeke make my heart race, and tingles rush through me from the memories but I'm still angry at him.

Miss you firefly
Wish I could lick and fuck your pussy right now

Wicked Temptation

I've let him linger on read for a bit, but he'll keep texting or worse FaceTime if I don't reply.

I can't face seeing his gorgeous face right now, so I text back,

Leave me alone, Ezekiel.

As I expected he's sitting on his phone, because his reply is immediate.

You don't mean that firefly

Don't call me that. I hate you.

No you don't, firefly

Urggh fuck off. I don't love you.

He doesn't reply then, and I throw my phone a little to hard on the bench when I sit down on the breakfast bar stool.

Mum is making bacon and eggs, and as usual can tell something is wrong when I let out a huffed sigh.

She turns to look at me.

"Morning Ava, what's up dear? You seem extra grumpy this morning."

I huff again, looking down at my phone on the bench.

"I miss him."

Mum is still glaring at me.

"Who? Drake? Didn't you break up?" she says, firing so many questions at me my head starts spinning and I don't know what to answer first.

"Yeah, but no, not Drake," I tell her, making myself look up at her as she slides a plate of greasy breakfast towards me.

"Oh then who dear?" she asks, handing me a knife and fork.

I cut into my bacon, lifting it to my mouth, and taking a bite as I mutter, "Ezekiel."

Mum looks surprised. Not shocked or worried.

"Oh. Did something happen when you visited the boys?"

I take a couple more bites of food, avoiding the question whilst I wonder if I should fess up. She wasn't mad about me losing my virginity to Drake, but Zeke is like a son to her, and even though she knows I love him I don't know whether she'll be happy about him being with me.

"Yeah mum and please don't be mad at me," I say, biting down on my lip a moment before shovelling in a mouthful of fried egg.

"Of course not dear."

"Good," I say hastily, gulping before continuing, "because I had sex with him mum and he didn't want me after."

Mum shakes her head. I'm worried she's angry.

"Oh dear, I'm sorry. Were you safe?"

I nod, feeling tears stinging my eyes when I reply, "Yeah but I love him, mum."

"I know dear."

"Ashton gets so mad though, so even without Zeke pushing me away we couldn't be together."

Wicked Temptation

Mum nods, letting out a slight laugh.

"Yes, dear, your brother is very protective of you. I'll talk to Ashton."

"Thanks mum. Telling him to lay off, especially now dad, um, Matias is around would be nice."

"I know Ava. And Matias would love to chat to you about these things to, and it's ok to call him Dad, Ava."

"I know mum. It just feels so strange."

"Yeah Ava, I understand, but he would love that, very much."

I nod, smiling and eating my last bites of food. Mum sips the coffee she's made.

"And Ava dear, maybe you need to tell Zeke how you feel or move on. I just want you to be happy."

"I know, mum. I will," I tell her, standing up and hugging her.

She kisses my hair and looking at her I smile, telling her, "I love you, mum. You're the best mum a girl could ask for."

"Aww, Ava dear. I love you to." I step back from the hug, and smile at her again as I head upstairs to shower.

I'm definitely lucky in the mother department. It's sad that my father was such an arsehole. I still can't believe he's gone. Dead. Not just around the corner in his castle anymore.

I don't miss him.

But I do miss Ezekiel Alessio, my Zekey bear. I just want to be in his arms, and hear him tell me he loves me.

Forty-One
Ava

Four Months Later

The last months have blown by, just like the sea breeze and even though I haven't spoken to him, Ezekiel *'owner of my damn heart'* Alessio he hasn't been far from my mind.

Wicked Temptation

Sometimes I've wanted to text him or call to tell him that I'm thinking of him. That I love him, but I'm to chicken to do that. And now I'm panicking because he's coming home with my brother, for Tempany's graduation and spring break before their last few weeks of uni for the year. I'm really nervous, so much so that I've thrown most of my wardrobe on my floor whilst looking for something to wear.

Eventually, I decide on a short sleeveless white floral motif lace dress with aqua bias binding highlights around the neck, sleeves and waist. It's cute, and with my hair down and a touch of mascara and lipgloss, I'm as ready as I'll ever be.

Zeke probably won't give me a second glance. For all I know, he's probably bringing Devney, as his girlfriend and I'll be back being Ashton's little sister.

Since the moment I walked into the auditorium with my family, I haven't stopped staring at Zeke; all day. It doesn't help that he's sitting with us and it makes it seem like he's family. It's nice his parents are here with mine, to show support.

I'm honestly trying not to stare at him across the table as we eat dinner, but as always his presence draws me in.

Tem touches my leg under the table and I turn my gaze to her.

"You ok, Av's?"

I nod, giving her a soft smile.

"Yeah, it's just hard seeing him after everything that happened."

"I get you, but do you still have feelings for him?"

I take in another bite of steak, before sighing. "Yeah, big time but he doesn't want to be with me. Every time I tried to talk to him he pushed me away and we haven't spoken for like three months."

Tempany laughs. "He's probably scared of getting another beating from Ashton. Does he know about what happened?"

"No, he'd probably kill him with his bare hands," I reply, laughing even though my words are true.

Mum had spoken to Ashton about not being as protective but I don't think my older brother listened. He still calls me every second day to make sure I'm not in any trouble.

"Yeah, maybe," Tempany replies laughing.

I smile back, excusing myself from the table to go to the bathroom.

Coming out after doing my business I find Zeke waiting for me. He looks so fucking sexy in black jeans, and a dress shirt with too many buttons open. It's so not fair that he can look so good.

My eyes can't help but scan his body, and my feet don't want to move so he pulls me into a hug.

I inhale his cologne, sighing and he murmurs in my ear, "I've missed you firefly." His words send a shiver through me.

So much for not being still affected by him.

He pulls back from the hug a little but still has his arms around me and his denim blue eyes are dark as they stare down at me.

"I've missed you so fucking much."

Wicked Temptation

"I've missed you to Ezekiel, but we can't," I tell him, not completing my sentence but he'll know what I mean.

We can't kiss. We can't be together.

"I know Av's, but please at least dance with me," he asks, not giving me a chance to reply before he continues, "It's a slow song. And I just want to be close to you."

I smile at him. I have no self control when it comes to Zeke, because I reply with a laugh, "Ok, but don't blame me if Ashton beats you up."

He laughs back, stepping back from me and admiring my dress as he takes my hand and leads me to the dance floor in the middle of the auditorium.

Lots of others are dancing but once Zeke has me in his arms and we're swaying together to the music I'm completely lost, only focused on him and his penetrative gaze that pulls me under and makes my heart beat like it's trying to escape a cage.

Caz May

Forty-Two

Ezekiel

Dancing with Ava, a thousand thoughts are tumbling through my head.

The main one is how much I'm in love with her. I want to let the words spill from my lips, but verbalising them now doesn't seem like the right time.

I also desperately want to kiss her. My body is responding to having her close again, with Z-man practically leaping out of my jeans he's so impossibly hard.

Wicked Temptation

I whisper in her ear, "Firefly, you set me on fire. I want to kiss you."

She murmurs, and Z-man throbs. "We can't Zekey bear."

I groan then, rocking my aching dick against her.

"God Av's...you know that nickname gets to me."

Leaning closer I bite her ear, and she pushes her body closer to mine. I swear I'm going to come in my fucking daks right now, so when the song finishes I drag her away from prying eyes.

Once outside I take her around the corner into the alley. It's dusk, and just enough light to see.

Kissing her hard and forcefully I push her up against the wall, my dick grinding against her. The kiss is hot, dirty and I can't get enough.

Her hands are all over me, and I grip her hair in a fist, yanking her closer so I can fuck her mouth, whilst our lower bodies scream for each other.

"Fuck Av's," I curse, breaking the kiss, completely breathless. "I'm sorry, but shit I wanna fuck you so bad right now."

She smirks at me, and fuck it kills me.

"I know. Me too, but we can't," she says softly, her pretty grey eyes on mine.

Her next words break my fucking heart, despite them being true.

"We need to move on, especially now with my brother around and tomorrow when we go to the beach."

I shake my head at her.

"Don't remind me. How I'm going to keep my hands off you when you're wearing a bikini is weighing on me."

She laughs then.

"Well, you'll have to," she jeers, poking me in the stomach in jest. I take a deep breath in, stepping away from her for some space because a hard, stabbing pain hits me in the chest, making me lean over in agony.

Ava is glaring at me, concerning painting her pretty face. "Zeke, are you ok?" She asks as though she's choking back a sob.

"Yeah, firefly I'm fine," I reply softly, standing up straight again, even though it's hurting like some motherfucker is squeezing my damn heart in a fist. "Just reflux from dinner."

"Are you sure?" She probes again, stepping closer to me.

I want to tell her, but at the same time I don't want her worrying about me.

I nod at her, smiling through the pain.

"Yeah, lets go inside and get a drink."

She smiles back, skipping away and calling out, "Ok, maybe wait a bit before you follow me. If you'll be ok?"

Again I nod, waving at her to go back inside without me.

"Sure firefly. I'll be fine, go..."

She runs back to me for a moment, crushing me into a hug and I give her a soft kiss on the forehead before slapping her butt when she walks away.

My heart is hers. And its breaking for her, because of her.

I need to let it heal or it'll completely break.

Wicked Temptation

Forty-Three

Ava

Since kissing Zeke outside in the alley after Tem's graduation dinner my whole body is aching for him.

I thought I'd shoved my feelings for him down inside me, locked them away so my heart doesn't ache for him. But boy was I wrong.

Caz May

Seeing him, touching him and kissing him and I want him again.

I've changed, thankful to be out of the dress and wearing only black knickers and a crop bra that barely holds my boobs in I flop down on my bed, and start scrolling through Instagram when a text message pops up from Zeke.

> Didn't get to say goodbye. You get home ok?

Yeah Zekey bear I did

I slap a hand against my forehead for typing his nickname. I go to delete it but he's already typing back.

> Loved kissing you tonight firefly

Back at you zekey bear.

> What are you wearing?

Not much.

> Oh come on Av's...tell me...are you naked?

Might as well be...I'm only in knickers and a bra

I can picture him groaning and a picture message pops up of him wearing tight white boxers. His dick is straining against the front, incredibly hard. I lick my lips, and type another reply.

Did I make your dick hard, Z?

> Of course you fucking did Av's.

Wicked Temptation

Mmm...wish I could touch you and fuck you again

Damn Av's...is everyone asleep?

Yeah I think so...why?

I'm coming over...now

Putting my phone down, I rush down the stairs and open the front door jumping up and down on the spot to warm myself up as the spring night air is cool.

Zeke is sauntering up the footpath, smirking at me. He's fucking shirtless, and of course the devil is wearing grey basketball shorts that show the outline of his dick.

Running down the path, I jump against him and he wraps his arms around me, kissing me.

Fuck, kissing him is heaven.

He keeps walking—with me still attached to him—to take me back inside, and once inside he puts me down. And gives me his signature sexy smirk.

"Hey to you to firefly."

"Hey Zekey bear. You look sexy."

His eyes trail my lack of clothes, before coming back to lock on my face.

"Sexy doesn't even being to cut how good you look in black underwear, Av's."

Caz May

I giggle, taking his hand to lead him upstairs to my room. It sends that familiar—and amazing—tingle through my body. He gets to me like no one else.

Creeping into my room, we don't say a word until we fall together on my bed, our lips meeting in a sweet kiss. He moans against my mouth, before pulling back and brushing my hair from my cheeks, his fingers caressing my skin. I want to tell him those three words, with his gorgeous full name to hear his reaction.

'I love you Ezekiel Stefan Alessio'.

Zeke looks heartbroken, and for a moment I'm scared I actually uttered the words out loud when it's clear he's not ready to hear them, but I know I didn't when he says, "Ava, I need to tell you something bad."

Shifting under his body over mine I move to sit up against the headboard. I'm not sure I want to hear what he's about to say, but I reply meekly, "Ok, I guess." I'm still worried i've blurted out my feelings for him.

He shifts to sit down next to me, his hand on my bare thigh. My skin heats at his touch, and looking across at him theirs pain evident in his eyes. Thoughts of earlier and the pain he was in after we kiss surface in my mind again. And I'm fucking scared. Scared that something is really wrong, and he's about to tell me goodbye.

"Ezekiel, please...you're scaring me."

"I'm sorry Ava. I um kissed Devney and went down on her."

"What? How could you, Z?" I question him, feeling tears sting my eyes. I wasn't expecting that.

"I shouldn't have Av's."

Wicked Temptation

"You don't say," I snap at him, not able to look at him because I'll fucking break. He's shattering my heart.

"Av's please, I'm sorry ok. I want you. You're my firefly."

"Don't say that Zeke," I tell him, still not looking at him, because I don't think I'd be able to without breaking into wretched tears.

The guy I love with my whole damn heart is stomping on it. "You said we can't be together. And then you sleep with Devney."

He grabs my jaw, suddenly but not forcefully and turns my face to look at his. His eyes have tears in them to. And it makes my heart beat quicken, because he's breaking telling me this.

"Firefly, I never fucked Devney. You own my dick now. And I'm so sorry I fucked up. You have to forgive me Av's, please."

He bites his lip, and fuck he looks so sexy. I just want to pounce on him, and strip him naked before riding him again, but I decide to make him suffer a bit longer.

"Why should I forgive you? You nearly slept with another girl, Ezekiel."

His eyes have a sparkle in them from me calling him Ezekiel. I know he hates his full name, but when I say it he's practically putty for me. And it makes me giddy.

He's still cupping my chin when he tells me, "It was stupid Av's ok."

"Really fucking stupid, Ezekiel," I taunt him again, licking my lips.

He groans, and it sounds so sexy, like he's so sexually frustrated he can't contain it anymore.

"You took my fucking heart with you when you left. I can't fucking live without you."

And my heart ignites with his words. Ezekiel Alessio might not be able to say he loves me. But he does, I'm sure of it. He's my air, my next breath, my every breath.

"I... I...can't breathe without you, Ezekiel." And with my declaration I take in a deep breathe, about to let the words, those words fall from my lips when Zeke pulls me closer, his breath mingling with mine, his forehead touching mine when he softly murmurs, "Mmm, Ava...I love it when you call me Ezekiel. Please....kiss me."

And I do. I kiss him to tell him I love him without words, getting as close to him as I can with clothes on.

Our bodies rock together and breaking the kiss I run a finger down his abs. He shivers at the touch.

"Zekey bear, I want you to fuck me again."

He laughs in that way that makes his whole body throb.

"Oh really, firefly?"

"Really, really, Zekey bear. And please I want to feel you, like really feel you."

"You want my dick in you bare, huh?"

I nod at him, smiling.

"Please, Zekey bear."

"Fuck Av's. Do you know what you're asking me, baby?"

"Yes, I got the pill."

"Serious?"

"Yeah, please Zekey, fuck me bare, now."

Wicked Temptation

I can't even think, as we kiss again. My hands fall to his waist, shoving his shorts down to find he's commando and his dick is hard. He kicks them away and I stroke his length. He groans against my lips, pulling back from the kiss. "Av's, your touch baby. It sets me on fire."

"You set me on fire to, Ezekiel," I taunt him, my tone lust filled.

"God, Ava. You're gonna kill me."

I laugh at that. "Well, get me naked and fuck me before you die, ok?"

He doesn't reply, instead he climbs over me, hooking his fingers into my knickers and sliding them down my legs. Impatiently he rips them, leaning over me to kiss my clit, before his tongue is making circles over my skin up to my boobs still confined in my bra. My whole body is aching for his touch, his lips on my skin. Freeing my boobs from the confines of the bra, he takes one his mouth, licking the nipple in circles, teasing me and completely setting my whole body on fire. I'm on the edge of desire just from this.

Breaking the contact with my heated skin, he smirks at me. "You're so fucking beautiful, Ava."

I don't know what to say back. There is no way I can describe how insanely attractive he is.

Gorgeous, handsome.

He's those, but he's more.

"Mmm, Ezekiel," I moan, cupping his cheeks to pull him close for a kiss. His dick is teasing me, at the edge of plunging inside me, and wrapping my legs around his butt I pull him in.

He moans against my mouth, before pulling back from the kiss, and cursing, "Holy fuck Ava!"

"Shh, Zekey bear. Someone will hear you," I tease, a finger against his lips.

He starts thrusting in and out of my core, and it feels fucking incredible.

"I don't fucking care, Av's. Being inside you, fucking you is fucking euphoria."

He pulls out for a moment, looking down between our bodies and slipping a finger inside me that he then takes between his lips and licks clean.

"Mmm, fucking delicious Av's. You taste like a wicked temptation."

"You're a devil, Ezekiel," I taunt him.

"Only for you, Ava Darby," he teases, kissing me and rolling our bodies over so he's behind me.

He's still kissing me, completely consuming when his dick slips back inside me. He rocks his hips against my butt, pumping his dick in and out as he kisses me, his tongue licking my lips and teasing me.

Breaking the kiss, I'm panting, breathless and sweaty. His touch, his body one with mine is the most amazing feeling in the world. I'm so close to falling over the edge. And nearly scream out my pleasure when his hand reaches down to flick his thumb over my clit, still fucking me so hard.

"Zekey, Zekey bear!" I scream out. "I'm gonna cum...fuck!"

He kisses me again, and I fall, my whole body spasming in release and warmth, as he explodes inside me with his dick throbbing as he comes with me.

Wicked Temptation

We lie there together, and he has a sweet smile on his face whilst he looks at me. He's making no move to separate our bodies and I don't want him to. I want to tell him. But instead I say, "I'm falling in love with you, Ezekiel. That was so amazing."

"Ava Darby," he murmurs, giving me a kiss again. "Every second you're in my arms is better than the last. But please don't ruin us with words we can't feel for each other."

He gives me a soft kiss against my forehead, slipping out of my body and standing up from the bed. I want to ask him to stay, to fuck him again and fall asleep in his arms but I know I can't do that.

He pulls on his shorts from the floor, and lays the blanket from my bed over me. He gives me a soft kiss.

"I'll see you tomorrow at the beach, firefly."

And he sneaks out of my room, taking my heart with him.

Caz May

Forty-Four

Ezekiel

Pulling up at the beach, my shitbox Nissan Skyline splutters as I cut the engine.

I can see Ashton, Tempany and Ava from the carpark. It's a fucking job to keep my eyes in my head, and Z-man tame in my boardies looking at Av's in her bikini, a pink and white striped triangle fabric number that her fucking delectable tits are spilling out of. Grabbing my towel and throwing it over my shoulder—after shoving my keys under the tyre rim—I head down the beach.

Wicked Temptation

Ava spots me, waving me over, and I take in the rest of the bikini. The bottoms are skimpy, and the damn top is pushing her tits together so much her cleavage is tempting me to bury my face in between the perfect mounds and lick the salt off her skin.

Fuck, I'm making myself hard.

Look, dickwad with hard on at the beach.

Throwing my towel down when I hit the sand, I revel in between my toes as I run to Ava, scooping her into my arms. My best mate is giving me side eye. I can feel his stormy eyes shooting lightning at my head, but I don't fucking give a shit. Having Ava in my arms—looking sexy as hell—makes everything not matter.

Ava is clinging to me, her barely covered pussy teasing the incredibly hard Z-man. "Av's, baby, you trying to kill me?"

"No, just checking to see if you still want me."

"Of course I fucking do, but you know hover brother is near. And I'm way to close to you right now for him."

She slides down my body, and I let out a loud groan before grabbing her around the waist and throwing her sexy petite body over my shoulder.

Stalking into the surf, I'm expecting to hear Ashton telling me to put his sister down and to stop being a wanker. But he's silent, locked in yet another PDA pash sess with Tempany. They're so fucking in love. He honestly needs to put a damn ring on her finger. To think back to the start of the year when he was going mental about Tem cheating on him seems so laughable now.

Caz May

Everything is falling into place—to be honest—and I need to find my damn balls to tell my best mate how I really feel about his little sister. Because it's fucking madness, but I've thought about having all the happy ever after shit--the endgame--with Ava.

Mansion by the beach, pool out the back that we can fuck naked in, and god, her with a rounded pregnant belly. I'm so whipped, so in love with Ava I want the whole damn world to know. She's mine.

She's screaming at me, "Zekey put me down!" , her feet kicking my chest and her fists beating my back.

I laugh at her shrieking, throwing her into the surf, and diving in after her. She comes up for air, and splashes me, spraying salty water over my face.

"Take that, Ezekiel!"

"What? You wanted me to put you down."

"You're a meanie, Zekey!"

"You're a cutie, Av's."

She sticks her tongue out at me, taunting me with the glint of her tongue ring that catches the sunlight. I love when it teases my tongue as we kiss. Feels so erotic.

Fuck, Z-man is throbbing.

I want to fuck Ava in the surf, with the waves rocking our bodies closer.

"Zekey?" she asks me, her eyes on me as we bob up and down in the waves.

"Yeah, firefly?"

"What you thinking about? You look a world away."

Wicked Temptation

"I was fucking you in my mind, Av's."

"Oh, was it dirty?"

"Damn straight it was dirty. Right over there against the rocks."

Her eyes light up with my words, and she looks towards the beach a moment before swimming over to rocky cliff face. She leans back against it, and close her in.

"Want me to fuck you here, Ava? With your brother watching from the beach?"

"Yes, Ezekiel. Fuck me..." she murmurs, her voice trailing off.

Swimming aside a little I find Ashton and Tempany are just behind us.

"Wanna not get so close to my sister, tosser," Ashton berates me, splashing me with a deluge of water.

"Just keeping her safe in the waves, arsehole."

"She can swim, dickhead," he taunts, grabbing Tempany by the waist and practically putting her on his dick as they swim next to us.

I turn back to Ava.

"Can you swim, Av's? Or you need my help?"

She laughs at me. "Don't know. Might need a big strong man to teach me."

Laughing I show her my arm guns, and grab her in my arms again, stalking in the water away from the rocky outbreak a little.

"Would you save me if I drowned, Ezekiel?" she asks huskily in my ear.

"Of course I'd fucking save you, firefly."

She giggles again, and I playfully throw her into the waves again.

Time stops.
She's gone.
I can't see her.
She's not coming up.
Panic hits me.
Where the fuck is she?
What the fuck have I done?

I start screaming out her name, "Ava! Ava! Fuck, Ava! Please Ava, fuck!"

She still doesn't come up for air. And I dive under the water, taking long strokes to dive down deeper into the dark water.

It feels like forever when I see her body—floating almost—limp near a rocky part at the bottom of the sand.

Scooping her up in my arms I kick frantically to the surface. And running out of the water I lay her down on the beach. Her whole body is cold, her lips as blue as the ocean. I can't fucking lose her.

I need her more than life.

Putting my head over her chest I can't tell if she's breathing or not. I'm scared fucking shitless when I bend over her more, straddling her as I start to resuscitate her, compressions on her chest, holding her nose as I breathe into her mouth.

Wicked Temptation

Nothing is happening. I'm going to lose her. I'll have killed my best mate's little sister, by being an fucking idiot. "Av's please!" I beg. "Av's, wake up please!" I'm still doing the compressions, trying desperately to give her my breath—true love's kiss—but it's fucking useless.

I can feel my best mate behind me and he grabs the waist of my boardies yanking me off of his sister and shoving me away. His eyes are darker than the blackest storm clouds. He's irate, furious, murderous. "Seriously! You motherfucker!" he bellows at me.

I'm struck stupid, looking between his arse about to murder me, and his unconscious little sister—my Ava—on the beach next to us.

"Fuck off, Ezekiel! You fucking cunt! You could have fucking killed her!"

I close my eyes, his words hitting me hard in the heart, as I run off without another word.

I've killed her.

Ava is going to die because of me.

Getting to my car, I grab the keys from the tyre rim, and get in, hastily speeding off to probably die myself.

Caz May

Forty-Five
Ava

Spitting out a mouthful of water I splutter and cough to find my brother standing over me. The look on his face is broken, completely shattered. My head hurts as I look around for Zeke. Being honest I can't even remember if he was even here. Everything seems hazy, and I'm absolutely fucking

Wicked Temptation

freezing even though the sun is beating down on me, and the sand I'm lying on is hot like ashes.

My brother gasps, as I try to sit up.

"Ash, what happened?" I ask when his arm wraps around my back to steady me. Dizziness fills my head. And Ashton is sitting on the sand next to me rubbing my back. My mouth feels weird to, like cotton balls have been shoved in it from the salt water. He's not saying anything and I'm really confused.

"Where's Zeke?" I softly ask my brother, regretting it the moment he speaks with so much malice.

"You nearly drowned because of him Av's!"

I'm not hearing that right. Zeke wouldn't do that.

"What? I was only under the water for like a second," I tell my brother, shaking my head and making my temples throb so much I wince a little.

Ashton shakes his head at me, clenching his fists angrily as though he's thinking about something that's making him irate.

"No Av's," he starts looking straight at me to make sure I'm listening. "He threw you in the waves and you didn't come up. You must have hit your head as well."

Clutching a hand to my head, I can feel a lump on the back and nod at my brother.

"Yeah, it hurts," I tell him before asking, "But where's Zeke now? Did he...?"

I don't even know what I'm asking. *Did he drown? Is he dead?*

I can't think about those things. If Zeke is gone and I'm still alive I want to get up from the scorching sand and run back into the ocean to drown for real.

Life without Ezekiel Alessio in it isn't worth living.

I let out a wretched sob, clutching my chest. My heart is going to break.

I love Ezekiel.

I need to tell my brother I'm in love with his best friend. But it's not the time, and when he takes my hand I bite back the words I was going to say.

"No Av's. I told him to leave."

"Oh, um..."

I'm shocked, and annoyed, realising that Tempany is standing behind my brother when she says, "An ambulance is on the way."

Shaking my head violently, making it hurt even more than before I practically yell, "I don't need to go to the hospital. I'm fine."

"I just want you to be safe Av's ok?"

I'm sure I'm fine. But Ashton won't let up so I give him a smile.

"Ok," I reply, sitting up and feeling a little dizzy.

Ashton stands up, helping me up by extending a hand to me and pulling against his side to hold me up. My whole body feels weak, numb.

All I can see in my head is Zeke's face, right before he nearly kissed me against the rocks. The sexy smirk, but also the absolute love he has for me. He hasn't said it, instead, he's pushed me away but from being with Zeke I know he loves me just as much I love him. And no matter what happens, I'm glad I got to be with him.

Wicked Temptation

Ashton looks to Tempany. "Thanks, Tem. Could you drive my car to the hospital when the ambo arrives?"

"Sure," She replies sweetly giving him a quick kiss. I smile at them, even though it hurts.

The ambulance is pulling up in the carpark, and with Ashton's arms around me, he helps me walk across the beach to the ambulance.

A jolt of pain hits me in the chest—near my heart—and I want to scream out and collapse to the sand.

Something is wrong.

Ezekiel has my heart in his hands. And I have his.

This pain is tearing me apart.

Something is wrong with my Zekey bear. I just know it.

Forty-Six

Ezekiel

The moment I get into the car and speed away from the beach the emotions consume me.

I'm going to lose her—my fucking firefly—the only girl who's ever had my heart and been able to ignite true feelings in my fucked up broken heart.

It fucking beats for her, breaks for her and it's completely fucking shattering for her and everyone we know.

I've killed Ava. I know I have.

Wicked Temptation

My hearts belongs to her, and right now the pain coursing through my arteries is the most excruciating pain I've ever experienced.

I've got tears streaming down my cheeks, my eyes puffy from crying and I can't fucking see straight, but I just want to get home to shower and collapse on my bed to block out this unbearable pain.

I shouldn't still be driving—especially at speed—but I know these streets like the back of my hand.

That being said, the trees that are now in my view seem new on this road. I'm wondering if I made a wrong turn, about to grab my phone from the seat beside me when I feel it.

The pain of my heart actually thrumming its last beat in my chest. And the impact of my car colliding with the trees on the side of the road.

My vision blurs, as I clutch my chest and let the darkness take me.

At least in death, I can be with my Ava.

I can't open my eyes. I can hear sounds, a constant beeping and voices in the room with me.

Everything in my mind feels hazy. And these voices sound familiar.

My firefly, my Ava is here, wherever here is.

My heart jolts, a harder beat in my chest when I sense more people coming in.

A familiar male voice says into the silence of this place, "Av's we have to go. Let him get some rest."

My heart hammers harder when another soft sweet voice whisper shouts, "I'm not going anywhere, Ashton. I'm staying with Zeke."

The air in the room shifts.

"There's nothing you can do now Av's. If he wants to wake up he will."

Ava is crying. I can hear her sobs. Her brother is breaking her heart. He's being a tosser.

I'm clearly in a hospital, dying and my so called best mate —brother from another mother—doesn't even a shit about me.

"How can you act like you don't care at all Ashton?" Ava questions her brother with a malicious tone. "You're best friends. Practically brothers. And you're acting like you don't even care if he ever wakes up."

The room is again silent, Ava's words hanging in the air. I want out of this damn headspace, to wake up and be like *'what you fuckers crying about?'*

But I'm still a dead weight on this wooden plank of a bed I'm probably lying on and my eyes are flicking furiously but I can't open my eyes. It's hell.

The silence is broken by a thunderous voice, "I do fucking care Ava! I'm scared fucking shitless!" He pauses, making my heart stop for a moment, and Ava lets out a wretched sob, before Ashton continues, his tone a little softer, "Which is why I can't sit here and wait all damn day and night."

Wicked Temptation

His feet scuffle on the floor, and Ava replies, "Well, go then. I'm staying with him."

My heart hammers harder in my chest. I'm alive. Ava is alive, and she's here, choosing me over her brother.

If I ever wake up, I'm telling Ashton I'm never going to be without Ava. She's my firefly who ignited my heart, and I'm so fucking in love with her I'd do anything to save her—be with her—even if that means my life is over.

"Fine Ava," Ashton snaps suddenly before his sneakers scuff the floor again as he walks out.

Ava is still sobbing and I realise someone else—most likely Tempany—is in the room too.

Hopefully, she will give some comfort to my girl because right now she's the only one here. And that breaks my heart.

Forty-Seven

Ava

T empany pulls me into a hug, and I sob into her shoulder for a moment.

I'm worried that Zeke isn't going to wake up. That I'll never get to be with him, again. It hurts so much.

Tempany breaks the hug, holding my shoulders when she speaks softly, "Av's...don't worry about Ash. He's just scared. And angry."

I nod at her, then shake my head pulling away from her a little.

"I know, but he doesn't get it."

"Get what?" she asks, her eyebrow raising at me.

"That I'm in love with Zeke. It's always been Zeke since we first kissed at my birthday last year, probably even before that if I'm being honest."

Tem smiles, nodding at me.

"He knows Ava," she tells me. "But Ashton is just trying to protect you. He doesn't want you to get hurt."

"I know," I reply, smiling as I think back to the events of the last year with Zeke. "But I know Zeke loves me too. He might not have said it but he does."

"Yeah, well hopefully he wakes up soon and you can tell him how you feel," she tells me with a sweet smile as she starts to walk out. "I'll leave you to it."

She walks out to my brother who's waiting outside for her. He pulls her against his side in a hug, kissing her hair softly and they leave the hospital together.

I want that kinda of love with Ezekiel but I'm probably not going to get the chance.

I'm shocked, stumbling on my feet when Zeke's parents come in, looking as though they haven't slept a wink this last week. I feel the same, as I've barely slept to with the headaches from my concussion plaguing me. The bump on the back of my head has lessened, and I was given the all clear to go home the day after. But I've barely spent a moment outside the hospital since though.

Zeke's mum, Lorraine steps up closer to me at the side of the bed.

"Ava, dear, how are you?" she asks, sounding a lot more chipper than her face shows.

"Hi Mrs Alessio," I greet her softly, wondering if I'm being to formal. "I'm ok. Just tired. And scared."

She nods at me.

"Yes, dear, so are we. Were you just leaving?" Her eyes dart to the door. "We saw Ashton on his way out."

"Um no," I mutter, biting down on my lip nervously. I feel like an intruder. "I want to stay unless you want me to go. I don't want to intrude."

I'm sobbing a little now and Mrs Alessio pulls me against her body into a warm hug. Her voice is soft when she says, "Oh Ava, dear."

"I'm sorry. I'm just scared of losing him," I mutter against her chest.

She kisses my hair.

"Us to dear." Pulling back from the hug, she gives me a look that has my heart hammering in my chest. "Can I ask you a question, dear?"

"Yeah sure," I reply, nodding even though I'm really nervous.

"Do you love my boy?"

I hiccup, loudly, swallowing them down in a big gulp to reply, "Um... I..." I can't get the rest of the words out. I haven't

Wicked Temptation

even told Zeke how I feel. I can't tell his mum that I love him with my whole damn heart.

She lets out a soft laugh. "Ava, it's ok if you do."

"Really?" I enquire, looking up at her from the floor.

"Yes, dear," she tells me with a smile that warms my heart. "Ezekiel is in love with you. He always has been. Probably before he even knew what love meant."

I'm completely floored. Hearing his mum tell me something about Zeke so openly makes me feel elated, and I know even though I haven't told Zeke the words I need to tell his mum.

"Oh um, wow...I...I love him too," I rush out, stammering on my words before adding, "But Ashton doesn't want us together."

She kisses my forehead. "Don't worry about your brother Ava. I'll have a talk to him."

I smile wide, my heart full when I reply, "Ok, and thank you."

"Anytime dear. You've always been the daughter I never had."

She hugs me again, and I cry into her shoulder for a moment.

Zeke shifts on the bed, murmuring as though he's waking up. His dad calls out, "Lorraine, look, dear. I think he moved."

I rush out then, squeezing his mum's hand and she nods at me.

If my Zekey bear is waking up I want him to be with family. And I want to tell him how I feel in person when I can kiss him until my lips hurt.

I'm so in love with Ezekiel Alessio—my Zekey bear—owns my heart and I'm just hoping he's ok, still my cheeky, sexy guy.

Forty-Eight

Ezekiel

Doctors come rushing into the room, the moment my eyes flutter open. Everything is all a blur, as they flit around me checking the monitors I'm plugged into.

Dad is next to the bed, holding my hand in his, and mum is on the other side completely shocked that I'm opening my eyes.

My heart sinks, that my firefly is gone. As much as I'm glad my parents are here, I wanted Ava's face to be the first one I saw when I woke up. I'd heard her words to mum, her telling

Caz May

my mum that she loves me. And I'd wanted to open my damn eyes that very second to confess that I love her to.

Dad breaks my thoughts by squeezing my hand and I look across at him when he says, "Hey son. How are you doing?"

Swallowing after yanking the breathing tube out of my mouth I let the words out in between breaths, "Good. But. Um. Shit."

For a moment I'm scared dad will tell me off for my language, but he doesn't.

"Understandable Ezekiel," he says with a nod. "We thought we'd lost you, boy."

"I'm s...s...sorry dad," I stammer, my voice husky.

"It's ok Ezekiel. But why so reckless son?" Dad enquires, an authoritative look on his face. I don't know what he knows and how much trouble I'm going to be in with my cop father.

All I manage to say is, "Ava."

Dad shakes his head at me, and looks across at mum who's still sobbing.

"But your heart son? Why didn't you tell us you were experiencing symptoms again?" Dad questions me.

I know I shouldn't have hidden what was happening from my parents, because the pain and turmoil in my dad's eyes and my mum's sobbing and laboured breathing is breaking my heart all over again.

"Because I didn't want to bother you, and I just thought I was stressed with uni and worried about what happened with Ava."

Getting all those words out makes my lungs hurt and I struggle to breathe for a moment, sucking in a few deep

Wicked Temptation

breaths before I ask, "What happened? I don't remember anything from after I left Ava at the beach."

"You had an accident, son. And the shock burst the artery. You had to have surgery again, and they nearly lost you."

"How long have I been out?"

"About a week. We thought we'd lost you," Mum says stepping closer to the bed and kissing my forehead.

"I'm sorry. I'm so sorry. But my heart, is it better?"

"Yeah, dear. The doctors repaired the artery and the hole. But you do need to be more careful and take blood thinners for a bit."

I nod, sitting up a bit on the bed when the doctors come back into the room. They fuss over me, checking the charts and disappear again to organise things for my discharge. I can't wait to get out of here and tell my firefly she has my whole heart.

Sitting at the dining table with my parents I'm shovelling mum's delicious spaghetti bolognese into my mouth like I've never eaten in my life when the doorbell rings.

I'm hoping it's my firefly.

Dad gets up, heading to the door and my heart both sinks to the floor and soars when my older brother is following my dad back into the dining room.

He nods at me.

"Hey little dufus. Glad you didn't die on me."

Caz May

Dad sits back down, and Dane comes in giving mum a hug when she stands up.

"Oh Dane, dear. It's so great to have you home."

"Good to be home, mum," he says coming around to my side of the table, and dropping his bag on the floor.

I stand up, and he pulls me into a side hug, scruffing my hair. "Scared the ever loving shit out of me, little dufus."

"Sorry D. But i'm here and you're here. I've missed you, bro."

"I've missed you to, little dufus and mum's cooking," he confesses, pulling his chair out so we both sit back down. Mum rushes off to get him a plate and he takes a strand of spaghetti from the serving platter on the table, putting it in his mouth whilst watching Dad giving him a chastising glare.

"So how long you staying for, son?" he asks Dane when mum comes back in with plate and fork.

Dane piles his plate with spaghetti before replying, "Only til Sundee. Just a short break before we're shipped off to separate bases for more training. I'm heading to Darwin for sniper training."

I gulp, choking on my mouthful of spaghetti.

"Shit, bro. Darwin and friggin machine guns."

"Yeah, little dufus, I'm gonna be a hot shot sniper," he says with a laugh.

We eat in silence then, just enjoying being together as a family.

Dane pats his stomach, smiling at mum.

"Best meal I've had in ages mum."

"No worries dear. It's good to have you home."

Wicked Temptation

He stands up then.

"Good to be home. If you don't mind though, I'm going go have a decent shower and turn in."

Our parents nod at him, and I stand up to follow him upstairs, to head to my room. He pulls me aside.

"You tell your girl, Ava, you love her yet?"

"Nope, bro. But I'm planning to on Sunday. Got something special planned."

"Nice, little dufus. Let me know if I need to kick ya best mate's arse to."

"Will do, but I've got it D," I tell him, giving him a fist pump.

"Goodnight, little dufus. Love ya ugly mug," he taunts, heading into the bathroom, as I head to my room.

My heart has never been so full of love. And I'm more than ready to tell Ava—my firefly—that I love her.

I gave into my wicked temptation and she's my whole damn world.

Caz May

Forty-Nine

Ava

Glancing at Zeke's text again my heart gallops in my chest.

Firefly, I'm taking you out for the day. Wear something sexy. Maybe no knickers.

Wicked Temptation

I'd only replied a winky face emoji and I've slipped on a blue strapless sundress, completely forgoing any underwear. I'm giddy just thinking about Zeke realising I'm naked under it.

Making sure I have my phone, and some cash I shove them into a small shoulder bag, pushing my feet into some black Havaiana thongs before I stumble down the stairs in my crazy haste to get outside to meet Zeke.

He's standing against a car on the curb, which must be his dad's. He looks delicious, wearing tight black shorts and a loose white t-shirt. I wonder if he's wearing jocks under the shorts, as I run up to him, enveloping him in a hug. It feels amazing to be able to hug him again.

I haven't seen him since he got out of the hospital a couple weeks ago. School had been winding down with exams, and getting ready for year twelve and I'd barely even had a moment to text him.

"Hey, Zekey bear. I missed you," I tell him, looking up at him with my arms still wrapped around him.

He kisses my forehead.

"I've missed you more, firefly."

I take a step back.

"So where are we going Z?"

He chuckles, sliding across the side of the car so he can open the door for me.

"It's a surprise, Av's. And damn you look fuckable in that dress."

I can't help the murmur that escapes my lips. Just thinking about fucking Zeke again has my core throbbing and desire dripping down my thigh.

Getting in the car, I clench my legs together, thankful the car has leather seats.

Zeke slides into the drivers seat, stirring the ignition and looking over at me as he drives off.

"Av's, you right, baby?"

"Yeah, fine. Why?"

"You look nervous. You don't like surprises?"

"Nah, I love surprises. But I um…"

"What, Av's?"

"I'm dripping all over the seat."

He laughs at my brazen admission.

"Fuck, Ava. Don't tell me that now. It's a twenty minute drive."

"Oh, I'm sorry," I mutter, biting down on my lip.

"Didn't you wear any knickers, Av's?" Zeke taunts, giving me his sexy smirk.

"No, I'm not wearing any underwear."

"Fuck, Av's. Fuck."

His arm moves across the console, and he authoritatively demands, "Open your legs, Ava."

I obey, letting my legs fall open and his hand slips underneath my dress. His thumb brushes against my aching clit, making me shift on the seat. I could come already, just from that simple touch. Another one of his fingers slips inside me, and he curses, "Fuck, Ava. You're so wet for me baby."

"Yep," I reply with a murmur as he withdraws his finger, putting it up to my lips a moment. My tongue darts out to lick it but he yanks it away and licks it himself, moaning.

"Fuck, Ava. Fuck, I wanna taste you properly again."

Wicked Temptation

"Soon, Zekey bear," I tease.

He groans in frustration and takes a turn down a dirt road. It makes me a little nervous, as I still have no idea where we are going.

"Z, please, where are we going?"

"You'll find out when we get there in like ten, little miss impatient."

I laugh, folding my arms across my chest. It pulls the top of my dress down, exposing my boobs more. And Zeke laughs at me.

"Av's, baby, please keep your clothes on until we get there. I promise you can get naked and have me all to yourself then."

"Fine," I huff, looking out the window at all the gum trees going by in a blur.

Five minutes later, Zeke pulls up the car in a clearing at the end of the dirt road. There's still trees surrounding us, and I'm honestly baffled about where we are.

He gets out of the car without a word, and is at my door before I can open it to get out myself.

Grinning he takes my hand, and helps me out, pulling me against his chest. Again he doesn't say anything, just kisses me, completely taking my breath away. I feel so overwhelmed with that kiss.

So happy, and so in love with Ezekiel Alessio that if I honestly died in that very moment, my life would be complete. No matter what happens from that moment on, I could be happy knowing I got to experience the greatest kind of love.

Breaking the kiss I sigh.

Caz May

"Zekey bear, you take my breath away."

"Oh, firefly back at you ten fold."

I laugh at his teasing.

"So is this my surprise? Bringing me out to the bush, and kissing me breathless."

"Yeah, nah," he replies shaking his head and stepping aside to the boot of the car. He grabs out an esky, and a rolled up picnic blanket. Hoisting that under his arm, and holding the esky in his grip, he takes my hand with his free hand, bringing it to his lips to kiss it when he says, "Come on firefly, it's just over here."

I follow him through a break in the trees, boggled when an expanse of crystal blue water surrounded by cliffs is in front of us. The sand at my feet is pristine white, and soft as silk when I kick my thongs off.

The grin on Zeke's face is wide, and contagious. Dropping his hand I can't help but grin to, running backwards on the beach and tugging off my dress to let it fall to my feet on the sand.

Zeke's eyes darken, and he drops the esky and picnic blanket on the sand before racing over to me, as I head the water's edge.

His eyes don't leave mine, even when he's hastily yanking his t-shirt and shorts off.

Just as I thought, he's naked to and his dick is hard already. I stop in my tracks, digging my toes into the sand as I stare at him, my Ezekiel, the protective, sweet teddy bear of a guy who completely owns my heart. Even if he doesn't tell me that he loves me, I need to tell him that I love him now.

Wicked Temptation

Again he grabs me in his grip, a hand around my waist, and one gripping my bare butt cheek. His forehead presses against mine and he whispers against my lips, "You're a devil Ava Darby Castello."

I don't verbalise a reply, don't let him say another word before I crash my lips to his.

His body crashes harder into mine, and I lick his lips, running my tongue ring along his lips which makes him moan into my mouth and kiss me harder. I can't wait another minute. I need to tell him.

I break the kiss, and look into his denim eyes that are almost black with desire; for me.

"Zekey bear...I..."

"Ava, please don't. Let me say something first."

I bite down on my lip, nervously shifting my tongue ring from side to side.

"Um...ok," I mutter.

He brushes my hair aside, his fingertips caressing my cheek, and his voice is soft but husky, "Ava Darby Castello, you're my firefly. You ignited my heart long before I could call you mine. And I'm completely, utterly, probably stupidly in love with you."

He kisses me softly, quickly before I can utter a word.

"I honestly love you so much, Ava," he tells me, not able to hide his smile. "Please tell me you love me to, firefly?"

"Of course I fucking love you, Ezekiel. You're my Zekey bear."

"Fuck, Av's. Say it again, please," he begs, staring at me intently.

"I love you Ezekiel Stefan Alessio."

He lets out a little laugh, his happiness overflowing.

"I love you more, Ava Darby Castello."

My heart fucking explodes. My Zekey bear loves me.

"Yeah? Show me how much you love me, Ezekiel," I taunt him, running off across the sand.

He grabs me around the waist from behind again.

"And how should I do that, firefly?"

I point across the beach at the cliff face of rocks.

"By fucking me up against those rocks over there."

He groans, laughing as he scoops me up into his arms, cradling me in them with a hand around my back, and his arm under my knees. I cup his cheek in my hand, kissing him.

Breaking it, he tells me, "I love you, and damn Av's I love it when you're dirty."

He carries me in his arms, over the cliffs where he puts me down and I lean back against the cold rock. He cages me in, kissing my lips quickly, before he falls to his knees and starts trailing kisses over my boobs, and across my stomach.

The cool breeze has my skin breaking out in goosebumps, but Zeke's warm breath and kisses trailing across my skin heat it and I nearly explode in pleasure when his tongue and teasing kisses reach my clit. He takes it into his mouth, plunging two fingers inside me at the same time. He licks me, fingering me and moaning so much it makes my body throb. I want to come for him.

I'm writhing against the rocks, shoving my core against Zeke's face, and I come, fast and in a gush over his face.

Pulling back, he stands up licking his lips.

Wicked Temptation

"Mmm, Av's you taste fucking delicious baby." I'm grinning at him, speechless. "You wanna taste, my dirty girl?"

I nod. He looks so fucking sexy. He puts his wet fingers in my mouth first, and with my eyes locked on his I lick them clean, murmuring. It's oddly arousing tasting myself on his fingers.

"Damn Av's. You're so fucking sexy." He kisses me then, taking my breath away and devouring my mouth, pouring all his love for me into the hot kiss. I can feel his hard dick teasing my entrance and tearing my mouth from his with a moan I tell him to, "Fuck me, please Ezekiel."

He groans.

"Fuck, Ava. Fuck." And he's inside me, filling me so deeply we're completely one. As he thrusts he pushes me harder against the rocks and it's so amazing. His lips find mine again, and he fucks my mouth as he fucks my sex.

Groaning again he breaks the kiss, pulling his dick out to just the tip. He grabs my waist and turns me around so my butt is in the air.

Taking a fist full of my hair, he stabs into me from behind, calling out, "Oh fuck, Ava. Fuck!"

Pushing my hands against the cliff, I rock my pelvis back and forth on his dick pounding into me.

The sex between us before was incredible but this—now we've admitted how we feel about each other—is beyond phenomenal. I don't want it to end. But at the same time I'm aching, climbing closer and closer to the edge.

Yanking my hair he pulls my back against his chest, kissing me hard, thrusting into with his release as I hit mine, moaning against his lips as we ride out the pleasure together. And then we're apart and he's gazing at me with bright eyes.

"You complete me Ava. I love you, no matter what happens."

"I love you to Ezekiel," I tell him, not sure what else I can say to tell him how much he truly means to me.

He grabs my hand, putting it against the scar on his chest. "My heart might have been broken already, firefly. But you fix it. My heart healed for you, Ava."

"Zekey bear, stop. You're going to make me cry."

"Sorry, firefly," he says with a soft laugh, and a quick kiss against my lips. "Let's go and eat our lunch for dessert. Then we can fuck again."

He winks at me, heading back over to the esky and blanket on the beach.

"Sounds good," I murmur, "But so does making love under the stars."

"Whatever you want, firefly," he tells me with a kiss, spreading the blanket out on the sand. "I'm going to make love to for the rest of my fucking life though Av's, just so you know."

I laugh at him, feeling giddy.

"Oh, are you proposing Zekey bear?"

"Not yet, Av's. But one day. I'm never fucking letting you go."

I kiss him again, and all thoughts of food are forgotten as our bodies collide with each other again.

Wicked Temptation

Fifty

Ezekiel

Gripping my guitar I head into the nursing home. It's been way too long since I've visited my Gram-grams. She was distraught about my accident, according to dad. I get it though since Pop died of a heart attack when he was fifty-five.

Grams is only in the nursing home because she often has falls with her osteoporosis getting worse.

At the front desk, the receptionist smiles, greeting me, "Well hello, Zeke. It's been a long time since we've seen you sweets. How're you doing?"

279   Caz May

"Hi, Elaine. And yeah I'm good. At uni in the city now. Just home for the holidays."

"That's lovely dear. I'm sure your gran will be happy to see you after your accident."

"Yeah," I reply with a nod. "All good to go on through?"

"Of course dear, they're all in the Rec room for arvo tea."

"Thanks," I tell her, nodding again as I head through the double doors into the main recreational area of the nursing home.

I spot Gram-grams immediately, and she hobbles over to me with the biggest grin on her face. Dropping my guitar at my feet I swoop her into a hug, kissing her hair.

"Hi Grams."

"Ezekiel, my lovely. You look better, sweetie."

"Thanks, grams. I'm feeling a lot better," I tell her as we head across the room to couches.

Sitting down, she can't stop smiling at me. "You gave your father quite a scare."

"I know. I should've told you all about my heart issues again. But I didn't want to burden you."

"I know dear. But your heart is precious. You've got a special one, and you need to be careful with it, in every way."

"I know Grams," I reply, feeling myself blush. I can't hide anything from my Grams.

"Ezekiel? Have you found yourself a girl?"

I nod, feeling giddy.

"Yeah, I have Grams."

"Tell me about her, dear," she says excitedly.

"Do you remember Ava?"

Wicked Temptation

"Ava Castello?" she asks her eyes lighting up as she gets all excited.

"Yeah, that Ava. I'm in love with her Grams. Finally told her I've loved her my whole damn life."

"Oh Ezekiel, dear, that's amazing. She's such a beautiful girl. Is her older brother, Ashton good with you being together?"

"No, not exactly. I haven't told him yet, but I will."

"I get that. His father was always a hot tempered man. Can't say I'm not delighted with the cards he got dealt."

"I know Grams. Ashton is better now without his dad around."

"Has he found a girl to?"

"Yeah, his stepsister Tempany," I tell Grams with a laugh because of the shock that paints her face.

"Oh, that's great. She was a sweet girl."

"Yeah, she still is. They're great together."

"That's wonderful dear," Grams says eyeing my guitar at my feet.

"Will you play us all a song?"

"Of course Grams," I reply, opening my guitar case as she calls over her friends.

Quickly I tune up my guitar and start strumming out a new song I wrote about Ava.

The words *'My girl, my firefly. You're the one who ones my heart,'* roll off my tongue with the melody.

Grams and her friends are all giddy and swooning over me. I strum the last chord, smiling when I put my guitar down, embarrassed and blushing.

"Oh Ezekiel, that was beautiful. Was that about Ava?"

"Yeah, Grams."

"Oh honey, that's just sweet," she says pinching my cheeks.

"Thanks, Grams. I have to go pick up some groceries for mum, but I'll see you soon."

"Ok dear," she replies to me.

I put my guitar away, hugging her again and giving her a kiss on the cheek before I leave.

Once outside I head down Main street towards the supermarket. I'm not watching where I'm going and bump into someone who is practically skipping down the footpath.

Looking up I'm shocked and happy to find that it's Ava.

"Hey Zekey bear," she greets me, hugging me. "What are you doing here?"

I give her a smile, telling her, "Visiting my fave person."

A sad look crosses her face, and she mutters, "Oh."

I laugh, pulling her close to whisper in her ear, "Other than you, firefly."

I want to kiss her, but a PDA in the middle of the main street in broad daylight probably isn't a good idea just yet.

"So who then?"

"My grams. Wanna meet her?"

"Yeah, sounds sweet."

Wicked Temptation

I take her hand, leading her back to the nursing home. When we walk inside I nod at Elaine at the desk, and she smiles wide back.

We head into the rec room again, and Grams spots me almost immediately again.

"Oh Ezekiel! She's even more beautiful than I remembered."

Ava blushes, smiling as I drop her hand and Grams crushes her into a hug.

"It's so lovely to see you again, Ava. All grown up and just beautiful."

"Thanks, it's lovely to see you to."

"I hear my Ezekiel here is quite smitten with you."

"Yeah, I love him to," Ava tells Grams, scooting closer to me and taking my wrist as she pushes herself to my side.

"Aww, dear, that's lovely. You're a beautiful couple."

"Thanks, Gram."

I give her another hug. She stretches up to whisper to me, "She's the one Ezekiel. She may be young but you're going to marry this girl."

I don't reply, just kiss her forehead before I head out with Ava still clutching my hand.

"What'd your grams whisper in your ear?" Ava asks as we start walking back down Main street together.

"Nothing, firefly, except that she can see how much I love you."

"Aww, Zeke, I love you too."

And fuck it, I give her a quick kiss before dropping her hand and following her as she continues skipping down Main street.

I follow her like a lost puppy dog.

I'd follow Ava anywhere.

Wicked Temptation

Fifty-One
Ava

*Z*eke is trailing behind me, following me down Main street like a lost puppy dog.

He's so cute. And I laugh when he catches up to me, stepping up behind me and grabbing me around the waist

Caz May

possessively. I love him showing affection like that. Love him showing everyone in Lockgrove Bay that he's mine.

Still attached to me we're hobbling along Main street, and he asks, "So where you off to anyway, firefly?"

"Quiksilver," I tell him, freeing myself from his arms, and smirking at him when I add, "I was going to get a new bikini."

He lets out a deep, sexy chuckle, giving me his signature smirk back when he says cheekily, "Damn Av's. I'd pay to see that."

I playfully poke him in the abs.

"Stop Zekey," I trill teasingly.

He laughs again.

"Oh, Av's. I've missed you this week. Can I come watch you try on the bikinis?"

I laugh and wink at him, loving how much my cheeky taunts get to him.

"Hmm...I don't know."

"You tease me, Av's," he jeers at me, grabbing me around the waist and walking behind me to the shop.

Once inside the Quiksilver surf store, he watches me with wide eyes that are darkening with desire as I grab bikinis off the racks.

Deliberately I taunt him, wiggling my butt as I head to the change room. Zeke follows, again like the lost puppy dog.

The change rooms only have a curtain close. Stepping into one and hanging up the bikinis I make a dramatic flourish of closing the curtain behind me when Zeke sits on the seat in front.

Wicked Temptation

Quickly I slip off my shorts, underwear and t-shirt. It feels naughty being naked in the change room, with Zeke outside. I can hear him breathing heavily, obviously thinking about me just behind the curtain.

I've put on a navy blue with white polka dots one and opening the curtain I step out to model it for Zeke. I cheekily give him a wink, posing sexily.

"Damn Av's baby," he says smirking and standing up. "You look sexy as fuck in that. But you know what?"

"What, Zekey?" I tease.

"You'd look sexier out of it."

I giggle, grabbing his hand and pulling him back into the change room and shoving the curtain across. I don't let him say anything, instead, I stretch up on tiptoes to kiss the sexy smirk off his face. He moans against my lips, shoving me against the mirror behind me, and sliding his hand into the bikini bottoms. I yank his shorts down, fisting his already hard dick in my grip. He moans into my mouth more, taking my tongue with his when he deepens the kiss.

Breaking the kiss, he shoves the bikini bottoms down to my knees, staring at me lustfully, possessively.

"I love you Ava, and you're the sexiest fucking woman on the planet."

"I love you to Ezekiel," I tell him, purring his full name by drawling out the syllables on my tongue.

"Fuck, Ava. You're going to kill me, baby," he groans, stabbing his dick inside me and thrusting hard.

His forehead is against mine, our bodies rocking together and it's so naughty I'm climbing towards my peak fast. Pulling back a little, but still thrusting into me, Zeke pushes the cups of the bikini top aside and palms my boobs in his hand.

"Fuck, Ava. Your tits are so perfect."

"Mmm," I moan, not able to think of a single word to say when having Zeke inside me—fucking my brains out—feels so amazing.

He kisses me quickly, before grabbing my hips as he pulls out so only the tip of his dick is at my entrance. He turns me around, gripping my waist to pull me back onto his dick. I steady myself with my hands on the mirror, rocking back and forth on his dick.

He gives my butt a cheeky slap, rubbing his hands all over my skin.

"Look at yourself in the mirror, Av's. Watch us fucking, baby."

I follow his demand, looking at the mirror, watching the pleasure on his face shown in the reflection. It makes my whole body throb, even more so when he grips my ponytail and yanks me back against his body to kiss me. His hand reaches down, his thumb flicking over my clit, and I explode in a rush, screaming out, "Oh shit! Fuck!" as Zeke pulls out and comes all over my back.

I hear feet on the floor, and a familiar voice call out, "Ava? Are you ok in there?"

Zeke is laughing and picks up another bikini to wipe the come off my back.

"Yeah, Braeden, I'm fine. Just tripped over and stubbed my toe."

"Oh, do you need some help?"

Wicked Temptation

"No, no I'm good. I'll be out in a sec."

I poke Zeke to stop him from laughing, getting the bikini off and putting my own clothes back on.

I grab one of the bikini's I didn't try on and head out of the change room after giving Zeke a peck on the cheek.

Braeden is standing just to the side of the change rooms, fixing a display. I hand him the bikini, and he looks at it oddly.

"I'll take that one, thanks."

I'm worried for a moment that I've given him the one covered in Zeke's come.

"Nice choice. You'd look hot in orange."

"Um, yeah. It's a good colour," I reply following him to the register.

Zeke stumbles out of the change room and comes up behind me. He gives Braeden dagger eyes when he stops next to the counter.

"Hi Brae," Zeke taunts, "didn't know you worked here man?"

"Recent, how's uni treating you?"

"Ripper. You killing with soccer?"

"Yeah, great man. And getting a bit of action off the field as well."

I'm intrigued by this conversation. I knew that Zeke would know Braeden, being a jock when he was at school, but this friendly banter between them is a little odd.

"Nice, man. Anyone I know? Or that Av's might know?" Zeke enquires as Braeden hands me a plastic bag with my new bikini in it.

"Nah, I don't think so. Ava and I..."

"Right, well good to know you're keeping ya hands off my girl. Have a good one, mate," Zeke tells Braeden, his tone rather malicious.

He takes my hand and drags me out of the shop, pinning me against the wall outside and kissing me, hard, passionately and unforgiving.

"Damn Zekey bear. That was a helluva kiss," I tease him, breaking the kiss and gazing into eyes that are boring into mine.

"Had to remind you that you're mine, Ava."

"Of course I'm yours, Zeke."

"Yeah, I fucking hope so Ava. I didn't like how Braeden was looking at you."

"Are you telling me you're jealous?"

"Yes, Ava. You're my girlfriend."

I give him a quick kiss, whispering against his lips, "Girlfriend huh?"

"Yes, Ava you're my girlfriend. And I'm not waiting another fucking minute to tell the world."

Again he takes my hand, kissing my forehead, and whispering in my ear, "And by the world, I mean your brother."

I laugh, smiling at him and squeezing his hand in mine.

We head down the main street, holding hands. And no matter what happens when we tell Ashton about us, I'm ready because Ezekiel Alessio is mine and mine forever.

Wicked Temptation

Fifty-Two

Ezekiel

Still clutching Ava's hand we wander into her house, straight into the rumpus room where my best mate is playing a video game with Tempany.

Loudly I speak, directed at Ava, "Av's, baby. Are you going to model that sexy bikini for me upstairs, in your bedroom?"

I give her a little wink, and she lets out a giggle.

"Sure, Z. I bought it to show you," she teases, dropping the plastic bag and stretching up on her tiptoes to kiss me.

It's barely a brush of our lips together when my best mate is practically flying off the couch, launching himself over the back of it and coming straight for Ava and me.

"Get your fucking mouth off my sister, arsehole!" he bellows at me, coming at me like an angry bear.

"Ash, man, calm ya titties. And no."

"No? You're telling me no?"

"Yeah, I'm telling you no. If I wanna kiss Ava, I'll be fucking kissing her," I tell Ashton, before giving Ava another quick kiss.

I can hear Ashton seething, practically hear his blood boiling as he's trying to contain his anger.

"What part of leaving my little sister alone don't you get?"

I laugh at his question, taunting him with my words, "I get it, Ashton. But doesn't mean I'm going to do it."

His attention turns to Ava. And she goes a little shy but stares her brother down.

"Av's?" he asks her, biting down on his lip, tongue-tied. Cheekily, I grab Ava's arse, giving it a little encouraging squeeze.

"Ashy, please just stop," she pleads her brother, waving her arms in the air. "I'm in love with Ezekiel and he loves me. We don't want to hide from you anymore."

He's glaring at her. And she's staring back at him.

He looks to me, his eyes softer.

"Is it true?" he asks, obviously wanting to hear me actually admit my feelings.

"Yeah, Ashton I'm completely in love with Av's. She's my girl."

Wicked Temptation

Still not happy with my answer, he asks, "How long? Have you fucked her?"

Ava scoffs next to me.

"Being honest, Ash man, I've been in love with her forever. Before I knew what the fucking word meant."

"And?" he queries, giving me dagger eyes.

I laugh to lighten the moment. I'm about to tell my best mate I've fucked his little sister. I kinda want to crawl into a hole and hide, but I need to tell him, and he asked.

"And yeah, of course, I've fucked her," I admit, pulling Ava against my side with a hand around her waist. "More than once actually."

Ashton guffaws. "Well, I can't say I'm happy about that, but I get it. And if you honestly love her as much as you're saying then I'm cool."

"Seriously? No more beating my arse if I look at her?"

"No, Ezekiel, but if you break her heart, or hurt her in any way I'll dig your fucking grave and shove you in it, alive!" He laughs hard then. And I follow, even though I'm scared shitless by his threat. I don't plan on hurting Ava; ever.

"Point taken, Ashton. And not going to happen. I'm all in, forever."

"Good, but please don't ever tell me details of you two together. A brother doesn't need to hear that."

We laugh together then, and I taunt, "Ok, so you don't want to know that we're going upstairs to fuck like bunnies for the arvo?"

"No! Fuck off Ezekiel!" he yells at me with a laugh.

"Well, we are, so don't come knocking," I taunt him with a laugh, taking Ava's hand as she grabs her new bikini from the floor at her feet.

Heading up the stairs I hear Ashton sit back down next to Tempany, and he's saying something to her before he kisses her.

I'm glad everything is out in the open. I can show Ava, and tell her how much I love her without hiding. And I do just that, stepping into her room, and pushing her against the wall by the door, just like the first time I kissed her.

"Remember our first kiss on your birthday, firefly?"

"Yeah, Zekey bear," she pants, her breath catching in her throat.

"I was already in love with then, Ava. I've always loved you."

She smiles at me, grabbing my t-shirt and pulling me close to kiss me. Leaning in I stretch my arms up above her head, kissing her deeper. She pulls back, and whispers to me, "I think I always loved you too, Ezekiel but I fell more in love with you with that kiss, and every kiss and touch after."

"Mmm, Ava," I murmur, kissing her again, and rocking my aching dick into her pelvis. "Say it again."

"What?"

"You know what, my love."

"I love you, Ezekiel. I love you so much, it hurts so good."

Groaning, I grab her around the waist, and she jumps into my arms. Heading to the bed, I slam the door shut, putting her down on the mattress.

Wicked Temptation

"Ava Darby Castello, I love you so much, my heart broke for you, and you heal it."

She pulls me down to kiss her, whispering against my lips, "Make love to me, Ezekiel."

I don't reply, just kiss her sweetly as I start to undress her, ready to make love to her now and until the day I die.

Fifty-Three
Ava

It's the last day of school, and sitting at the bleachers I'm absentmindedly watching the soccer team playing the final game of the year.

Braeden is kicking the ball, heading straight for goal, but his eyes are elsewhere, looking towards the bleachers where some others from our year level are sitting.

Wicked Temptation

I wonder for a moment if something is going on there, but shrug it off when Dakota shrieks at me, "A, are you even listening to me?"

"Yeah, you were saying...um...sorry I tuned out."

"Of course you did," my best friend says with a laugh. "You're daydreaming about your sexy boyfriend."

I guffaw at her. My innocent bestie just said sexy.

"Kota, you feeling ok?"

"Yeah, better than ok. Why?"

"You just said sexy."

"So?" she questions with a laugh.

"Well, I was kinda thinking about Zeke yes, but yeah. What were you saying that has the word sexy on your mind?"

"I kinda met a guy."

Again I guffaw at her. And I'm looking at her like she has two heads.

"Really? Do I know him?"

"Well no, and he's not a guy. He's a man."

"Kota! Tell me!"

"He's the new vet. And he's gorgeous." I'd heard about a new vet in town, and trust my best friend to have already met him. She probably stalked him by taking one of her menagerie of animals there.

"Trust you to have already met him. But isn't he like old?"

"No, well I don't know. He's older, but maybe like thirty."

"Dakota Abigail, really?"

"I know, Ava, but when I looked at him outside the vet clinic, he, gosh he made me feel all tingly."

"Oh I know, Kota. But please be careful."

"I will," she tells me, smiling. "So what were you thinking about before?"

"Oh nothing. Just wondering if something is going on with Braeden and Ariel."

"Yeah," she agrees, nodding. "Something weird is going on there."

"Yep," I agree, standing up to run down the bleachers when the final bell goes, and the crowd of students goes wild with Braeden kicking a last minute goal.

"I'll catch ya later, Kota. Zeke's taking me out for an end of year celebratory date."

She laughs at me.

"Got ya bestie. Code for sexy times."

I poke her in the arm.

"Who are you? And what have you done with my bestie?"

"She's here. And is becoming a woman."

"Weirdo, love ya face," I call back to her, running down the bleachers to my boyfriend who is now waiting for me at the bottom.

I don't hear Dakota say anything back, as I jump into Zeke's arms and kiss him.

"Hey Zekey bear," I greet him, peppering kisses over the stubble on his jawline.

"Hey, firefly, happy to see me, huh?" he teases.

"Always, Ezekiel. But only because I love you."

"Yeah, well I love you more, Ava. And this arvo I'm taking you that place," he tells me with a wink as I slide down his body to my feet.

He takes my hand and leads me out to his new car.

Wicked Temptation

Getting in the passenger seat I can't help but smile at him, watching him as he steers the car with one hand out into traffic and to our beach.

The beach where we confessed our love and made love under the stars. I'm already giddy—and turned on—just thinking about being in my Ezekiel's arms again, making love to him until I die.

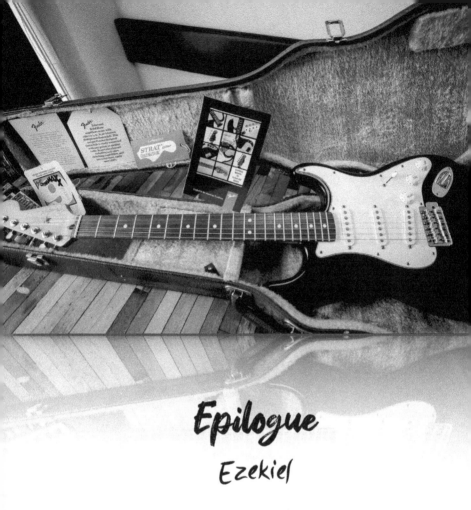

Epilogue

Ezekiel

Four months later

It feels like some alternate universe, sitting on a barstool sipping beer surrounded by our family, and friends at Ashton and Tempany's engagement party.

He'd gotten a bit of slack for proposing to her so young, but they're it. One of those couples who grew stronger apart and Tempany lives with us now having started uni. She's doing

Wicked Temptation

teaching at Deakin with Ashton, and seeing them parading their love around the house makes me want to chunder and makes me miss Ava so much. I can't wait for the year to be over so she can come to shack up with us in the city too.

Ashton and I are looking at the girls, Ava, Tempany, Dakota, and another girl I remember from school, Ariel dancing like idiots in the middle of the room. They all look so happy, and it makes me beyond happy to.

Taking another sip of beer I smile at my best mate.

"So much has changed, huh?"

"Yeah, crazy," he replies, gulping down his beer.

"I can't believe your fucking engaged man."

"Me either, but wouldn't take it back for anything. I love Tem so fucking much."

"I know man. You're the perfect couple. She makes you a better man."

"Don't get all sappy on me, Zeke."

"Can't help it. Love makes us all saps."

"Yeah, still can't believe you fell for my shit of a little sister though."

"Yeah, you don't know her like I do though," I tell him, realising how crazy that sounds the moment the words leave my mouth.

Ashton laughs, replying, "And that's a good thing because that would be a crime."

"Yeah, but honest man, I love Ava and I'm going to marry her one day."

"I know. At least wait until after her twenty-first though."

"Fine, I'll wait three years if I have to." I laugh and hold up my empty beer bottle towards him. "Want another?"

"Nah, I'm going to dance with Tem."

He walks towards the girls on the dance floor and I catch eyes with my girl, my Ava. She runs over to me, kissing me as she practically climbs me.

"Av's, baby. Your parents are watching," I tease.

"Don't care, Zekey bear. I love you, and love kissing you."

"I love kissing you too, firefly," I tease, leaning close to inhale the sweet gardenia smell of her perfume. "And I love fucking you to."

She giggles at me, squirming a little in my arms. She looks up at me, worrying her lips between her teeth.

"What were you and Ashy talking about?"

"Oh nothing," I tell her winking.

"Didn't look like nothing," she teases me back with a soft kiss.

I love that we don't have to hide how we feel about each other anymore, especially in these moments when I get to see her after months apart.

"Fine, I was telling Ashton that I'm going to marry you, firefly."

"Oh, bet he loved that," she replies with a cheeky smile.

"Yeah he told me I have to wait until you're twenty-one, but if I could I'd marry you yesterday."

"Promise?"

"Yeah, Ava Darby. I love you so hard, baby."

"I love you more, Ezekiel Stefan," she says with a teasing tone that stirs Z-man in my black jeans.

Wicked Temptation

"Keep that up, Av's and I won't be able to stop myself from having my wicked way with you."

She kisses me again, and I melt into her kiss, into her soft body against my hard body.

She was my wicked temptation, and now she's my forever.

Giving in to temptation was the best thing I've ever done.

Australian Slang Glossary

Ute-Truck

Bludger- someone lazy, doesn't do much and possibly relies on social security benefits

Ripper- something really good/great

Ridgy-Didge- Cool

Bonzer-Great, awesome

Pash/ing/ed- to kiss/make out

Arvo- afternoon

Chunder- Vomit, throw up

Gobby- Blowjob

Aussie Kiss- going down on a girl

Daks- pants/trousers/underwear

Undies/Knickers/Jocks-underwear (female knickers, male Jocks, undies both)

Dakking/ed- to pull or have pulled someone daks down (see above)

Bathers- universal name for female swimwear

Budgie Smugglers- small male swimmer that looks like underwear (google this one to see)

Thongs- Footwear, otherwise known as flip flops

Esky- Cooler-you keep drinks cool in it

Dunny- toilet

Bogan-white trash/trailer trash

Old Fella- Your father/Dad

Wicked Temptation

Franger- Condom, Trojan etc

Milo- a malt chocolate powered drink mix (can be made hot or cold)

Macca's-MacDonalds

Fair Dinkum- used to emphasise or seek confirmation of the genuineness or truth of something

Fucking/Bloody oath- similar to above, but an extreme or emphasised way of saying yes.

Shark Week/Rags- A woman's monthly cycle

Stuffed if I know- a nicer way to say fucked if I know

AFL- Australian Rules Football

Giving me a view of her breakfast-

Stalk Me

Instagram- @cazmayauthor

Facebook- @CazMayAuthor

BookBub-Caz May https://www.bookbub.com/profile/caz-may

Spotify- cazcat25

Website- https://cazcat25.wixsite.com/cazmay-author

Goodreads https://www.goodreads.com/cazmay

Wicked Temptation

Acknowledgments

Hey lovely readers!
Thank you so much for reading another book of mine.
I truly love sharing my words with you all.

My biggest shoutout goes to my writer bestie, one of
my soul sisters in life, Tina Lee. She helped make this
the best book it can be, and wrote the bonus chapters
with me as well (in the ebook if you want to read). I
can't put it in words how much her support and love
means to me. Writer besties for life, girl!

And to my amazing street team ladies. Thank you for
reading, and sharing all your amazing reviews and
teasers. And being there for me when I'm in a slump,
thinking this is not worth my time anymore.
You all lift me up and I appreciate every single one of
you. Thank you for putting up with my crazy and being
on this crazy book journey. I hope you stick with me,
and love every word I give you to devour.

As always I need to thank my hubby, Cam. He's my
rock, even when he's a dufus. And my fur babies who
give me countless late cuddles when I'm up writing
and editing.

And my other bestie, B. I hope you loved Ezekiel's
story as much as Ashton's. Your words of support

Caz May

amaze me and I can't thank you enough for always being there for me.

If you've enjoyed this story, then please review on Amazon and any other platforms you can.

Thanks again to all of you!
I love you all and appreciate each and every one of you!

Signing off! For now!

Caz May xx

Wicked Temptation